THE BIRTH OF ZETA-PLUS

There was a dull thud—like a thunderclap far away. Bob rushed to the window and looked at the garage. Smoke was pouring out of the door; this time it was black. There was a terrible smell. The Pop Stretcher had blown its top! He ran down the stairs and out of the house.

In a few seconds he was standing at the entrance to the laboratory-garage, surveying the damage. One by one the youngsters from the area charged up and joined him, panting and wide-eyed.

The Pop Stretcher was destroyed. It was spread all over the floor, walls, and ceiling of the garage in the form of broken glass, wires, nozzles, and a thick, drippy, gooey liquid that smelled like overcooked chow mein.

Bob didn't know it, but it was the dawn of a new age for progress. And the beginning of a whole mess of troubles.

BOB FULTON'S AMAZING SODA-POP STRETCHER

An International Spy Story
by
JEROME BEATTY, JR.

Illustrated by Gahan Wilson

A BANTAM SKYLARK BOOK

TO THE MEMORY OF *JIM ADAMS*

BOB FULTON'S AMAZING SODA-POP STRETCHER
A Bantam Book / February 1979

ISBN 0-553-15056-1

Published simultaneously in the United States and Canada

PRINTED IN THE UNITED STATES OF AMERICA
0 9 8 7 6 5 4 3 2 1

Contents

1. An Unusual Invention

Peeling an onion one warm summer afternoon, and staring intently out through the kitchen window, Mrs. Fulton watched the ferryboat *Clermont* chugging its way across Barnstable Harbor toward her. At the wheel, she knew, was her husband. In a few minutes, she also knew, there would be a crashing and bumping which would mean that the sixty-four-foot steam vessel would be tying up at the dock at Phinney's Lane, just a few feet from the Fulton home. Sometimes the landing was so violent that the windows in the house rattled.

"Twenty-two years, four round trips a day," she recalled as she watched, "and he still can't bring her in properly. Oh, well." Tears came to her eyes as she thought fondly of her husband, and as she continued peeling onions.

A screen door screeched and a thin, pretty little girl with long blond hair slunk into the room and grabbed the refrigerator door. She was wearing sandals, red shorts, and a half-buttoned blouse which was only partly tucked into her waistband where it belonged.

" 'Lo, Mom."

"Good afternoon, Jennifer."

Jennifer opened the door wide and leaned upon it, eagerly running her blue eyes up and down and sideways over the refrigerator contents.

At this point Mrs. Fulton's jaw dropped and she cried, "Why, that's strange. Your father is taking a short cut inside Buoy C-ii, and the tide is low. I do hope he doesn't run aground again. Oh, dear, why is he taking such a chance?"

"Probably because of the smoke," Jennifer muttered, still hanging onto the door of the refrigerator.

Mrs. Fulton turned to face her daughter. "Jennifer, how many times have I told you to stop holding the icebox door open? Close it immediately. What smoke?"

"Mother, how many times have *I* told *you*: re-frigerator, not icebox. The smoke in the garage. I guess Daddy can see it from the boat." She took one last glimpse of all that food, slammed the door, and began picking over some fruit in a dish on the kitchen table.

Mrs. Fulton wiped her hands on her apron and rushed out down the back steps, calling back, "Well, young lady, if the garage is on fire, you certainly don't seem very upset about it, I must say!"

Jennifer shrugged her shoulders and peeled a banana.

As the worried woman approached the scene, she found that sure enough there was a cloud of white smoke pouring out of the wide-open doors of the garage and up into the blue sky. Not only that, but a crowd of neighborhood children were standing there watching.

"Oh, those foolish things!" she cried. "They'll be burned to a crisp!" She grabbed a watering can half full of water as she dashed across the driveway. "Stand back!" she ordered. In her hurry, she tipped the can as though she were watering some thirsty geraniums and pushed through the throng. With that, they scattered, for Mrs. Fulton was sprinkling water all over their bare heads as she forced her way into the garage.

"Hey, lady, whatcha doin'?" one surprised boy shouted.

"Gee, Miz Fulton, you got my dress all wet," whimpered a girl.

The rest of the boys and girls moved quickly away. The woman found herself inside the garage with an empty watering can in her hand. But she could see no flames. Instead, her son Bob was standing there in his bathing trunks, covered with soot and grime from head to toe. The smoke was pouring from some sort of small furnace in the middle of the garage floor.

"Robert Fulton," his mother asked grimly, "just what is going on here? Now, is this building on fire or isn't it?"

"Of course not," the boy replied. He took the can out of her hand and moved closer, speaking softly so the other kids couldn't hear. "But please don't call me Robert, will ya, Mom?"

She jumped back. "Don't come near me. You're a mess." She looked around at the contraptions, tools, machines, wires, and huge amounts of useful and useless junk that filled the garage. This was Bob's "laboratory," where he dreamed up and put together the inventions and experimental projects that took up so much of

*Sprinkling water all over their
bare heads . . .*

his time. The Fulton automobile wasn't kept in the garage any more; there just wasn't room. The reason it didn't freeze in the winter was that Bob had invented a Motor Warmer for it.

Mrs. Fulton, relieved that there seemed to be no danger, pointed to the smoking gadget. "Well, then, what is this?"

"Oh, that?" Bob bent to poke the fire. "That's my Pop Stretcher." He grinned proudly at it. "Been getting up steam. Little too much damper or something. Smoky, isn't it? Don't worry." He twisted a handle and the smoke died down.

His mother studied the machine carefully. It made no sense to her at all. Above the little firebox was a tank. From it came a number of squiggly tubes and pipes, leading over to a huge glass bottle and back again. There were many faucets and knobs and instruments. They stuck out all over.

"Want to see how she works, Mom?"

She nodded, thinking to herself, "I must show an interest in the activities of my children."

"Well," the boy said, as his eyes brightened and he turned to the contraption, "I know it sounds funny, but what the Pop Stretcher does is to make your soft drinks last longer. I'm using Coca-Cola in it now, so now it's stretching Cokes. Get it, Mom?"

"Land's sakes, I'm not sure I get it."

"You could use malted milk or orange pop or anything. Now, here's what we do." Bob opened the shiny brass cover of the tank, grabbed a large sack off a nearby shelf, and poured its contents in. "Fifty pounds of sugar."

Mrs. Fulton screamed. "Fifty pounds of sugar!"

But Bob wasn't listening. He had run outside and grabbed the garden hose, which he attached to one of the nozzles on the tank. "Plenty of water!" he yelled, as he ran around to the side of the house to turn it on. Mrs. Fulton saw liquid start to move through the tubes. Air hissed from an open valve. Bob ran back.

"Now we add the important stuff," he said. He went to a shelf where about a dozen cheesecloth bags sat in a row. He took one. "Inside here," he held up the bag, "is what I call Ingredient Zeta. I mixed all these bags last week. There's sassafras root, cornstarch, ginger, oyster sauce, lemon rinds, and so forth. I can't remember all I put in. We use one bag each time." He then hung it inside the tank with a wire hook.

"One more thing," he continued, while his mother stood there in utter amazement. He took a bottle of Coca-Cola from a case sitting on the ground nearby, opened it, and poured the con-

7

tents into the huge glass jar. He then capped the jar, closed the tank cover, twisted a few knobs and handles, and stood back, rubbing his hands together. The Pop Stretcher boiled and fizzed.

"May I ask a question, son?"

"Sure."

"What does it do?"

"You see this big glass jar? It holds about twenty gallons. Well, after a few hours of distilling, fermenting, and boiling, it will be filled with something that tastes pretty much like Coca-Cola. So I get twenty gallons of Coke for the one little bottle I poured in. That's pretty cheap, isn't it? Look behind you, Mom. See all those kids standing there?"

She turned around and saw the neighborhood throng blocking the door again. For the first time she noticed that each of them held a cup or glass of one sort or another. Their eyes were shining.

"Fellas, it's starting to drip!" one of them cried. At these words, the press became greater. Bob went out to calm them down.

"All right, in line, just like the last time," he ordered. They obeyed, and he returned to his mother's side. "They test the product for me. I charge them a penny a cup, just to keep it businesslike. Of course, the stuff won't be ready for a

He twisted a few knobs and handles . . .

long time, but they get so thirsty for it they come early."

Bob's mother gave him and the Pop Stretcher an admiring glance. "Well, I do declare. Imagine supplying the whole town with soft drinks, all from one little bottle of Coke."

"Last week I did it with Seven-Up."

"You are a clever boy. There's one detail that isn't very clear to me, however."

"Just tell me what it is, Mom. I'll explain it to you."

"If it takes fifty pounds of sugar, and all those other ingredients in your recipe for the little bag—do you realize how much a bottle of oyster sauce costs, Bob?—then I am not quite sure that it wouldn't be cheaper just to buy the Cokes in the bottles rather than to stretch one in such an expensive way. Have you figured out *exactly* how much this machine costs to run? And did you take all those things out of *my* kitchen?"

Bob shifted uncomfortably. "Why, Mom, I haven't really had a chance to do any careful accounting of—say, isn't that Dad coming home?" He was glad to change the subject.

They both heard the familiar creaking and groaning of the Phinney's Lane dock which meant that Captain Fulton was guiding his vessel to a landing. "Shiver me timbers!" they heard him cry, as the boat hit the pier with a tremendous crash.

"Well, I've got to get back to my dinner," Mrs. Fulton said. She pushed her way through the mob of thirsty kids and went back to the kitchen. "Fifty pounds of sugar—Pop Stretcher—my goodness! I wish he'd invent me an automatic dishwasher one of these days," she thought to herself. From the window she watched the crew tie up the boat. Some passengers got off and started up the lane toward town. Finally Captain Fulton came down the gangplank and stomped toward home. The *Clermont* had completed another voyage.

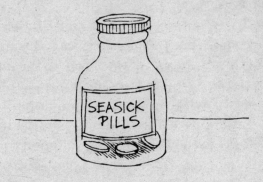

2. A Terrifying Explosion

"Avast, ye landlubbers!" roared Captain Fulton as he entered the yard. "Where in blazes is the fire?" He stomped toward the garage. Captain Fulton stomped exactly as though he had a wooden leg, but both limbs were as sound as those of an Olympic athlete. In fact, his legs were as healthy as his right eye, which was covered with a black patch.

You see, Captain Fulton, who had been skipper of the ferry between Phinney's Lane and Sandy Neck for twenty-two years, was a very bad sailor. He often felt woozy, crossing the two miles of smooth water known as Barnstable Harbor.

He carried a pocketful of seasick pills, which he gulped when he thought no one was looking.

More than once he had run the *Clermont* aground on a shoal, because he could never remember which side of the buoys marked the channel. Sometimes he would run down to his cabin and quickly thumb through his *Pilot's Guide to Eastern Waters* and look it up. "It's red on the right returning, and that means black on the left going out—no, black-right-out," he would say to himself.

He was usually saved trouble when a passenger would shout and point, "Hey, Captain, the other way!"

Captain Fulton had never sailed on any waters but the harbor, except for the foggy days when he would miss the Sandy Neck landing completely and go right out into the broad expanse of Cape Cod Bay. As a boy, he had grown up on a farm in Kansas, but had come to Barnstable on Cape Cod right after graduation from agricultural college. The town needed a ferryboat captain very badly, so they had hired him.

To cover up his weakness as a sailor, Captain Fulton over the years had grown a beard, put on the eye patch, stomped about on a stiff leg, and acquired a lot of other seafaring habits. He was

13

always shouting "Sail ho!" and the like, and his language was considered salty.

But he was such a fine, delightful gentleman that nobody minded. Everybody pretended he was the best ship's captain since Sir Francis Drake. His crew admired him, and they did most of the work.

"Clear the deck!" he ordered, as he pushed his way past the boys and girls at the garage door. "Man the pumps! Break out the hoses!"

Bob met his father, saying, "It's all right, Dad." He explained the situation to him.

"Well, lad, ye had me on edge. I saw the smoke and put on extra canvas to get here. Glad it's nothing to worry about."

As the two stood there, the Pop Stretcher boiled and bubbled. Slowly the huge glass container was filling with a dark liquid. The children were pushing and shoving for position.

Finally Bob grew impatient and spoke to them. "Look, kids, this won't be ready for a long time. The ice isn't even here yet. Why don't you all go and play for a while? Go on, now, shoo!"

There was much grumbling, especially from the boys at the head of the line. They didn't want to lose their places up front.

Bob's father then shouted, "I'll tell ye what, me hearties! Ye go on home and get your passports

"Clear the deck!"

The children were pushing and
shoving for position.

stamped by your mothers, and I'll let ye ship out with me on the five o'clock cruise to Sandy Neck!"

There was a cheer from the gang, and they raced off in all directions.

"Always like to have the little shavers on board," Captain Fulton explained. "Makes for a happy ship." He smiled as he and Bob walked toward the house. The Pop Stretcher hissed merrily as they left it.

"Bob, I want to have a word with you," his father said seriously. "Would you report to my quarters at about eight bells?"

The boy looked up at him. "All right, Dad. Eight bells—that's four o'clock isn't it?"

The man's eye twinkled. "You know full well it's four o'clock, son."

Captain Fulton and Bob were as close as a father and son could be. Each had a sense of humor and made friends easily. It was a good thing, because there was one point on which they did not agree. Bob's ambition was to be a scientist; his father wanted him to go to sea. But because they respected each other, and because each had a pleasant disposition, they did not argue about it.

But they talked about it a lot. At eight bells Bob

reported to his father's room, and the Captain brought the subject up again.

"Last summer, you recall, we made a little agreement. Instead of signing on the *Clermont* during vacation, you cleared out the garage and made your laboratory. During the winter, when we scraped her bottom, you were too busy to help. Now this summer you are still landlocked."

Bob listened politely. His father continued, removing the black patch for emphasis. His two clear blue eyes focused on his son. "Our agreement was that you would launch yourself on a scientific career, or else give it up and join the ship's crew during school vacation. So far, lad, you haven't done either. You've put together a few gadgets, but——"

"A few gadgets, Dad? What about the Motor Warmer? That makes it pretty easy for Mom to get the car started in winter."

"Aye, but——"

"How about the Scarecrow? Every farmer in Barnstable County, practically, has one."

The Self-Starting Scarecrow was one of Bob's most remarkable inventions. Most crows, of course, are not scared of a scarecrow. Instead, it is a convenient spot for the lookout bird to sit and caw his "All Clear." But by a clever arrangement of weights, pulleys, and gears, Bob had made a

The Self-Starting Scarecrow

scarecrow that—when a bird landed on it—flapped its arms and moved its head. Two flashlight batteries supplied the power. Bob had already earned $104 building and selling Self-Starting Scarecrows in the Cape Cod area.

Captain Fulton smiled. "Aye, that scares the pesky critters to a fare-thee-well. But how about your marks this year? This lab took up so much of your spare time, you weren't able to steer a true course in the classroom."

"Gee, a C average isn't all that bad. And another thing I could mention. How about the Automatic Pilot I installed in the *Clermont?*"

Captain Fulton leaned back and roared. "Ho! Ho! Ho! Scuttle that talk, m'lad. What makes you think old Cap Fulton would ever be usin' that confounded doodad? I leave that for those young greenhorns who take the helm when I'm on shore leave."

Bob looked rather unhappy. "Well, all I can say, Dad, is that if you understood science the way you understand the sea, you'd know that a scientist has to experiment and experiment. That way he gathers knowledge which helps him find the answers to unsolved problems."

"What about this Cow Catcher? What answer will that give you, except to supply cheap lemonade to the neighborhood?"

"Pop Stretcher. Well, it—I'm not sure, but maybe it will show how—" Bob stopped, as a whistling noise was heard through the open window. It grew louder and louder until it seemed as if a jet plane were passing about two feet over the roof of the house.

Bob jumped up and cried, "That's the safety valve!"

Before he could move, there was a dull thud—like a thunderclap far away. He and his father rushed to the window and looked at the garage. Smoke was pouring out of the door; this time it was black. There was a terrible smell.

"Come on, quick! The Pop Stretcher's blown its top!" the boy yelled. He ran down the stairs and out of the house. His father fumbled to put on his eye patch. He grabbed his brass-buttoned uniform jacket and cap and thumped after his son.

In a few seconds they were both standing at the entrance to the laboratory-garage, surveying the damage. One by one the youngsters from the area charged up and joined them, panting and wide-eyed. Some of them carried their cups and glasses.

No one spoke for a couple of minutes, and then one boy whined, "Gee whiz, that's the end of the Pop machine." A few voices echoed "yeah" and "gosh." They were a sad little group. Bob Fulton was the saddest. The Pop Stretcher was destroyed. It was spread all over the floor, walls, and ceiling of the garage in the form of broken glass, wires, nozzles, and a thick, drippy, gooey liquid that smelled like overcooked chow mein.

"Looks like the valve got jammed," the boy scientist remarked.

His father looked about. "Well, young fella-me-lad, you really stretched that Coke. Ho! Ho!" He roared with laughter. Even Bob had to smile slightly, though he didn't feel like it.

Just then there was the sound of a gong. Captain Fulton started. "By the Great Horn Spoon!" he cried. "Two bells! Time for the evening ferry. How many of you landlubbers are coming along?"

Half a dozen boys and girls raised their hands and followed the skipper across Phinney's Lane to the dock, where they clambered aboard. Bob heard his father shout, "Single up, fore and aft!" He then turned to the task of cleaning up the mess left by the explosion.

On a front porch not far away, two ladies sat in rocking chairs and knitted. From there they could see across the lane and through the trees to the busy scene of action at the Fulton garage.

"Looks like the valve got jammed."

Even with the loud noise and smoke, however, they did not stop rocking or knitting.

"Just another explosion in that boy's madhouse," the one named Annie commented. "Some day he's going to blow us all sky high."

"Or his father will run his boat right up to this front yard and frighten us to death," joked the other, Ingrid.

"Handsome devil, though, isn't he? With that beard and all," answered her friend. They both laughed and laughed, as they knitted and rocked.

3. Some Serious Events

In his laboratory Bob did his best to straighten things up. The Pop Stretcher was a complete loss, except for a few items that could be salvaged, such as a faucet here or a fitting there. The most he could do was to shovel and sweep the debris into a pile and dump it into a barrel of trash in the corner. He worked a long time to restore order, but without too much success. He found that every last corner—wall, ceiling, and floor—was covered with a layer of thick, gooey, sirupy material.

The explosion had plastered this goo onto and into the tools, a wheelbarrow, an old wrecked bicycle, the license plates nailed to the walls, the sleds, the pot stove—literally everything that was stored in the large, two-car garage, whether it was old junk or new equipment that was a part of Bob's scientific experiments.

Talking to himself, Bob mused, "When the tank and bottle blew up, this stuff was inside, I imagine. It must be the raw material that stretches the Cokes. Ugh, it sure smells horrible! I'll clean it tomorrow."

A crashing noise and shouts of warning indicated that his father was bringing in the *Clermont,* so Bob returned to the house, where he took a shower and got ready for supper. Jennifer was helping her mother set the table. Soon the Fulton family was seated around it, where young Bob did his best to make small talk so that no one would bring up the embarrassing affair of the explosion.

He paused for breath once too often, however, and his mother blurted out, "Captain,"—she always addressed her husband that way—"you've just got to do something about that situation in the garage." She put the corner of her napkin to her eyes and sniffled a bit. "It seems to me I've got enough to worry about, with you making that perilous crossing on the water each day, without

26

"Captain, you've got to do something about
that situation in the garage."

having to fret about when my house will be blown up."

"Oh-oh," Bob thought. "Here it comes."

He was right. Captain Fulton looked up. "Son, far be it from me to fire a shot across your bow when you're making full steam for your objective. I've been as fair as can be about your ambition. But today's catastrophe proves what I was tellin' you earlier: you're on the wrong tack. I'll have to put me foot down and order you to duty aboard the *Clermont* for the rest of the summer. You'll have to forget this scientific twaddle and come to sea, where you're needed." He took a bite of hardtack.

Bob placed his knife and fork on his plate. "Aw, Dad, I may be on the trail of something big. You have to accept these scientific experiments for what they are—a means to an end."

"What end d'ya have in mind, lad, scuttling Phinney's Lane?"

"Well, I for one can think of an end to all this foolishness," Mrs. Fulton put in, "and that is for Robert to clean up that garage so that we can put the car back where it belongs."

"Mom, please don't call me Robert. I've asked you."

Jennifer piped up, "And put my bicycle there,

too. I'm tired of having to leave it outside where it gets rusty and everything."

"Listen, brat, you never put your bike away before," her brother snapped, "so why would you be doing it now if the garage was open?"

"Children, children," cautioned Mrs. Fulton, "let's not get excited over nothing. I've been putting the bicycle away most every night when it looked like rain. Fact is, I just tucked it away there yesterday when I saw some clouds in the sky. And I do wish you'd remember to take care of that yourself, Jennifer, instead of my having to——"

"You *what*, Mom?" Bob interrupted, seeing vividly in his mind the picture of the wrecked bicycle in his lab. "You mean that old heap that got blown up is Jennifer's new——"

"In the explosion?" Captain Fulton was asking.

"My bike!" Jennifer screamed. She jumped up from the table and ran out.

"What old heap?" Bob's mother asked him.

"Well, there's a bicycle in the garage and it's ruined, that's all. I figured it was the old one."

"I gave that old one to Nanny Vonnegut months ago, Robert Fulton," she declared. "If there is a two-wheeler in your laboratory, it's the

29

three-gear Sussex Speedster that Jennifer received for her birthday and it had better not be ruined, that's all I have to say, young man."

"Aw, Mom. Don't call me Robert. The name's Bob."

"You were christened Robert."

Captain Fulton looked up from his plate of slumgullion. "Lad's full handle is Robert Farragut Fulton. If'n you landlubbers had any sense, we'd be callin' our son Farragut, like I ordered long ago. But no, you're as stubborn as a granny knot in December."

Mrs. Fulton's gray eyes softened and the corners of her mouth crinkled. "*Your* name is Robert," she said gently. "And you called your first ferryboat *Clermont* after your name-sake——"

Her husband pointed dramatically as he replied, "So it be, but my name is not Robert *Farragut*. When I was born, in the swayin' fo'c'sle of a clipper rounding the Horn, there wasn't none of this fancy middle-name folderol, you can wager."

Bob spoke, with a mouthful of food. "I thought you were born in Junction City, Kansas."

His father looked wonderfully blank. "Junction City, *where?*"

Before the discussion could go any further, it

was brought to a sudden halt by the high-pitched return of Jennifer.

"My bicycle's ruined," she wailed. "It smells and it has two flat tires!"

The Fultons jumped up and streamed out the back door to the garage.

"It's all covered with something aw-w-ful," Jennifer bawled, as she brought up the rear. And it was. The family stood in a little knot and stared at the mess that had once been a Sussex Speedster with three gears. The explosion seemed to have wrecked it.

"Wow," was all Bob could say, realizing what had happened. He scratched his head.

Jennifer blubbered on. "Look at that! And I have to go on a picnic with the Brownies to Craigville Beach Saturday, and we're supposed to ride bikes! Booble-ooble-ooble-oo!"

"Knock off the confounded squalling," ordered her father. The girl quieted down as her mother pulled her close.

"For goodness' sake, Ro—er—Bob," Mrs. Fulton said sharply, "why did you have to do a thing like this?"

"Gosh, Mom, I didn't know it was in the garage. Besides, I didn't put it there. And if you weren't always going around straightening up and putting away—why, this bike would be out in the

Bob felt responsible for the damage done to the Sussex Speedster.

driveway, leaning against the stoop, where she belongs."

"That's what mothers are for, son," she observed, mostly to herself.

In spite of his defensive reaction, Bob felt quite responsible for the damage to the Sussex Speedster. He bent to inspect it. In addition to the flat tires, the fenders were out of shape, the chain was loose, the rubber on the handlebar grips, on the pedals, and on the brake shoes was burnt and shredded. The once proud two-wheeler was in bad condition.

"This bike is rusty," Bob finally mumbled, glad to find something for which he was not to blame. "Certainly that's not my fault. Somebody must have left it out in the rain."

"In the driveway, leaning against a stoop, where she belongs—I suppose." His father wryly echoed his son's previous remark.

"Well, *really!*" Mrs. Fulton burst out. "I just can't win in this family. Leave something outside, it gathers rust. Put it away, it blows up. Either way, mother is wrong."

The men had to smile at this. Unfortunately, Jennifer saw nothing funny. She jumped up and down and hit her fists against her hips.

"Just what are you laughing at?" she demanded, starting to booble-ooble all over again. "How am I going to the picnic?"

The ear-splitting howls brought the others to their senses. Captain Fulton put his hands on his hips, studied the smashed two-wheeler, and pronounced his son's fate. "This does it, me hearty. Into the deep six goes your ding-fangled laboratory. Y'can belay all this inventin' and experimentin' till the summer's over and we can see what your schoolwork looks like. In the meantime, startin' Monday I do a little lab work of me own."

Mrs. Fulton looked up, startled. "Oh? What could that be?"

"Start changin' this lad into a deckhand. Ho! Ho! That's an experiment for you!"

Now it was Jennifer's turn to smile. Bob considered his father's joke a bad one. "What about the bike?" he asked listlessly.

His father stopped his laughter. "I've got that one worked out, too," he announced. "We need someone with mechanical ability, the tools, and some knowledge of the workin's of such a rig—a reliable local fella who'll start immediately and get the job done before Saturday."

"You're right, Dad," agreed Bob. "An expert, in other words, who can devote the next few days

She started to booble-ooble all over again.

to Jennifer's bicycle and nothing else. And you have someone in mind, do you?"

"Aye. His name's Robert Farragut Fulton."

4. Repairing the Damage

The next morning, after breakfast of dried fish, Captain Fulton made his way toward the dock and the first sailing of the ferry for Sandy Neck. As he passed the garage, he was pleased to note that the doors were ajar and to see the figure of his son inside. He stopped. Deep within him, the man understood and sympathized with his son's scientific yearning. It was simple enough to compare it with his strong desire to go to sea when he was that age himself. He had, he remembered, disobeyed his own father's wishes in that respect.

"Just imagine," the Captain reflected, "I'd be

raisin' wheat instead of steam if'n I'd done what Pappy wanted."

So, although he didn't mean to force his son into a mold which he did not fit, he still hoped to make sure of two things: how good or bad a sailor would Bob really be, and was his inventive streak just a stage he was going through?

"After all," he thought, as he peered into the garage, "a few mechanical gadgets don't launch an Albert Einstein. If'n the lad's got the makin's of a great oceanographer like Matthew Fontaine Maury, I'd like to know about it."

The scene inside the building grew sharper as the Captain's eye became adjusted to the darkness. There was the would-be inventor seated on a bench, picking at his fingernails and staring at his feet as he kicked his heels into the grime of the floor. The bicycle lay there, broken and bent, a dramatic reminder of the previous day's holocaust.

Captain Fulton spoke. "What's this, mister? Haven't cast off yet?"

Bob looked up gloomily. "And I'm not going to, because I don't know where to start and I don't know where to finish. I'm not a bicycle expert, like you think. I'm going to take this heap over to Al's Repair Shop. He's the expert. I'm just trying to figure out now where the money's coming from. I know *you* won't give it to me."

The father's beard seemed to twitch. He put his hands on his hips and for once appeared at a loss for words. Finally he breathed, "Well, I'll be a busted backstay! You sure jibed, didn't you? One minute all set to put Tom Edison to shame and the next, not even able to tackle a simple task like this." He pointed at the bike.

"It's not that I'm unable," Bob protested. "It's just not my—not my—"

"Not your speed, lad, not your dish? Is that it? What was it you were telling me about a means to an end, about experimentin' and experimentin'?"

"With a *bicycle*?"

"Now listen to me, lad," the Captain said, severely but not unkindly, "you can't be choosin' your experiments to suit your taste, just pickin' the ones that are fun and droppin' the ones that are work. When I was your age, I caulked many a leaky skiff with frozen fingers and pumped many a dirty bilge, when I thought I should've been at the helm of a trim schooner bound for the Caribbee. But it didn't hurt me a bit, I found later."

Bob waved a hand at the bicycle. "I can't caulk this."

Despite this ridiculous remark, his father felt the lecture might be taking effect. "It may interest you to know," he went on, "that the bicycle is the most-used form of transportation on this here globe. Blimy, I've seen thousands of Orientals pedalin' their way through the streets of Mandalay. I've seen an Egyptian farmer pumpin' his rice paddies full of precious water by means of a dee-vice constructed from a bike in worse condition than this one here. I've watched one of them natives rig a bike to his outrigger and scoot across the South Sea lagoons like a crazy porpoise."

Bob had never heard of rice paddies in Egypt, but he made no comment. He was more interested in the outrigger illustration; the idea appealed to him. He wondered where his father had learned about these things.

"Say," he said brightly, before the Captain could go on, "what about trying something like that here in the harbor? A couple of surplus wing tanks, a chain and sprocket gismo——"

His father shook his head. "Someone's already thought of that. Pedalboats, they call 'em. But my point seems to have made a dent in your skull, am I right? A bright lad might learn something useful even from a lowly two-wheeler, you'll admit that?"

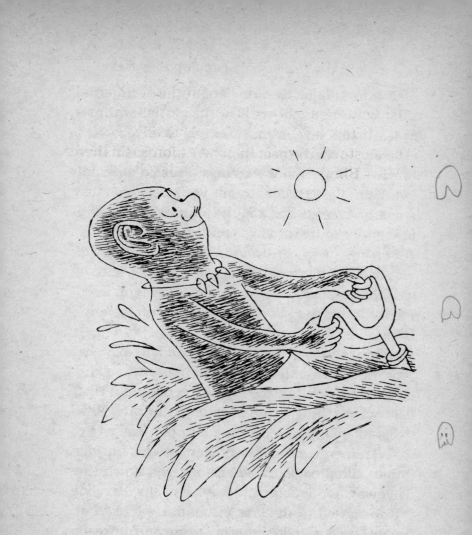

*He was interested in the outrigger
illustration.*

Bob was silent, thinking about the outriggers. Finally he nodded his head in partial enthusiasm. His father continued emphatically.

"Now, if you be headin' for Al's Repair, it'll be for two new tires and whatever else you need for overhaulin' this machine so's your sister can use it again. As fer the cost of the materials, it'll have to come from your wages on the *Clermont*."

Bob knew when he was licked. He stood up. He was dressed in an old T-shirt, blue jeans, sneakers, and no socks. He stretched. "All right, Dad. I'll try to fix the bike, but I don't promise anything."

"That's the boy!" exclaimed the Captain, clapping Bob's shoulder and stomping out.

"But it's sure not the type of experiment that leads to anything," Bob declared grumpily. "If it does, I'll swim to Sandy Neck under water."

"I'll remember that rash statement, m'lad," his father called back, as he disappeared down the driveway.

Bob turned to the task at hand. He looked at the Sussex Speedster, talking to himself. "Needs new tires. Oil the chain. Repair the broken link. New pedals, brakes, seat. Clean up rust. Paint fenders . . . two wing tanks and a crossbar. Attach the chain and sprocket to——" He grinned.

"Pedalboat, hey? Why I could run my *own* ferry, for kids or something."

As usual, Bob's mind had wandered in the direction of another newfangled scheme. This time it was the pedal-powered outrigger, and for the next two days, while he worked on the bicycle with his hands, his brain was working on the other. As a result, you couldn't say he did the best repair job in the world.

Nevertheless, he was busy all that day. He rushed all over town, obtaining supplies—paint, oil, tires, etc. Then he got to work. First, of course, he had to wipe off the gooey residue resulting from the Pop Stretcher explosion. He really gave it only a lick and a promise, then threw the dirty rags into the trash barrel. He removed the rust with kerosene; he shined and cleaned the rims and spokes; he replaced the grips on the handlebar as well as the broken seat and pedals. He rewired the front and rear hand brakes and tested them. The chain was adjusted and the tires were pumped up, and Bob was finished.

"That'll get by," he thought, as he stood back and admired what he'd done.

The vehicle was upside down on the workbench, resting on handlebars and seat. Bob gave the front wheel a push, watching it spin as he wiped his hands with a rag. A moment later he left for dinner, after closing the laboratory doors.

At the table, Jennifer asked the inevitable question. "Did you fix it?"

"Yup."

"Oh, boy!" she cried. "Let's see it."

"Not yet. Tomorrow I'll paint her. It'll take a day for the enamel to dry properly. I'd say that by Friday morning you can have her."

"None too soon," Mrs. Fulton remarked dryly.

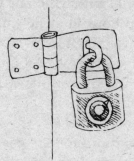

5. A Mysterious Affair

Early the following day Bob unlocked the doors to his lab and walked in. As he got ready to work, he noticed something strange. The front wheel of the bike was turning, slowly, to be sure, but turning. He put his palm on the tire and brought it to a halt.

"Hey, who's been in here?" he said out loud. He called toward the house, "Hey, Mom, anybody been in the garage?"

She answered through the screen door of the kitchen. "Certainly not, son. Everyone's still upstairs."

Bob scratched the top of his head. "That's funny. Well, I'll get the painting done."

He opened and stirred the two small cans of red and white enamel with which he would decorate the bicycle. An hour later he was finished. The rest of the day was spent in "swabbing the deck," as his father had ordered. All manner of equipment and scraps of various kinds had to be cleaned and put away. By afternoon the place was in fairly good order.

"Now there's room for the car," Bob thought regretfully, as he realized his lab days were over until further notice. "And my last big project— fixing a busted bicycle. Not a bad job, though." The Sussex Speedster was still upside down on the bench. It looked good compared to what it had been. Absent-mindedly Bob gave the front wheel a push; it spun easily. He did the same for the rear; it turned quietly.

As he prepared to leave, he recalled how a wheel had been moving when he opened up in the morning. He wondered how any intruder could have gotten inside the place without a key. The windows were not bolted, but they were jammed tight from never having been opened. If someone was nosing around the lab, Bob thought, they must have picked the lock. There was one way to stop them. He removed the old padlock from the door and rummaged in his toolbox until he came up with one of those foolproof jobs where you need a combination. He carefully turned the knob and opened it.

"No one knows the secret to this one but me," he reminded himself, as he closed the big doors and snapped the lock on the hasp. He twisted the little dial and pulled at it to test it. He went to wash up. At the supper table he announced that the paint was dry and that Jennifer's Three-Gear Sussex Speedster was ready for action again. Everyone was pleased.

Bob tried to sleep late Friday, but he was roused by an excited Jennifer. "Come on!" she cried, as she shook her brother. "The garage is locked and no one can open it and I want my bike and——"

"Okay, okay, quiet." Bob dragged himself out of bed and went downstairs, yawning and pressing his hands against the walls for support in his sleepy condition. At the garage he put the knob through the combination—right, left, right—and pulled open the doors. What he saw jolted him into full consciousness.

The wheels of the bike were slowly turning!

It was impossible!

The bewildered boy stood there in a daze for a moment, until Jennifer's squeal interrupted his thoughts. "Oh, boy!" she gushed. "Can I have the bike now?"

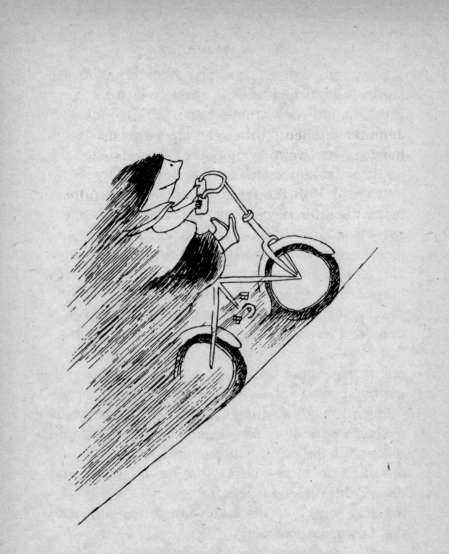

"She's going awfully fast!"

Bob placed it right side up, and the two wheels stopped their slow movement when they hit the ground. "I guess so," he replied, in rather a fog. Jennifer jumped on the seat, gave a push with her foot, and went flying down the driveway.

"Whee!" she screamed.

"Gosh," Bob thought, "she's going awfully fast." Jennifer turned up Phinney's Lane and sped away. Bob ran out to watch her. To his amazement, it appeared that she was coasting along without pumping—uphill! Then he heard his mother's voice.

"Robert Fulton! What are you doing in the middle of the street in your *pajamas*?"

As Bob ran in to get dressed, the words kept pounding inside his head: "I've *got* to find out what this is all about. I've *got* to find out!"

Bob pulled on his old blue jeans and T-shirt, opened the bottom drawer of his dresser, and reached underneath a pile of sweaters, pulling out a tin box. Then he went to his closet, reached up over the door on the inside, and felt around in the dark until he found a tiny key hidden up on the door frame. With the key he opened the tin box. Inside the tin box was a wallet with four rubber bands around it. He pulled them off, opened the wallet, and poked through a pile of private papers he kept there—a note from a girl in

49

school, a ticket stub from the first circus he ever saw, John Glenn's autograph, and many other treasures—until he found what he was looking for, the combination of the padlock. It obviously had not been disturbed since he put it there a year ago. Besides, he had altered the numbers by adding his own lucky number eleven to each of them: where the directions read seventeen, for instance, he had made it look like twenty-eight. So, even if some thief did have this (the one and only written combination), it wouldn't open the lock, because the instructions had thus been sabotaged.

But this discovery didn't help Bob; it just deepened the mystery, for it offered no explanation of how the bike could have been tampered with overnight. He carefully put everything back, finished dressing, and returned to the garage. He checked the screws that held the hasp—still covered with dust and paint—it was obvious that they hadn't been removed. He looked at all the windows—closed as usual. He sat down on the stool and added up all he knew about the case.

"No one enters the door or the windows; no one is inside; the wheels are turning when I lock up at night; the wheels are turning when I come back in the morning." The boy leaped to his feet.

"It's got something to do with the bicycle! I've got to see that bicycle! Where is she now?" He hurried outside and into the street. No Jennifer. All he could see were Ingrid and Annie sitting there, knitting, on their front porch.

"She went that way," one of them told Bob, when they heard him calling. They both smiled. Bob thanked them and went back to his onetime laboratory, to wait for the girl's return. It seemed forever, but was probably only a few minutes, before he heard a familiar rattle and saw Jennifer skidding to a stop right at the door.

"Wowee!" she cried as she jumped off the bike. "You really fixed this fine, Bob. It just flies along."

Bob grabbed the bike. "Say, lemme look this over a bit, will you?" Jennifer followed Bob as he pushed the Sussex Speedster into the garage. There he upended it once more on the bench, placed a hand on the front tire, and gave the wheel a slight little push. It moved slowly. He did the same with the other wheel, and backed up to his stool without looking away from the vehicle. The wheels moved slowly, slowly, slowly. Bob sat there and watched them intently.

Jennifer was silent for a while, then made a face. "Say, what d'ya think you're doing, any-way?"

"She went that way."

"Well, if you really want to know," Bob answered, not taking his eyes off the bike, "I'm trying to figure out why these wheels were spinning this morning." Suddenly he turned his head to stare at his sister. "Hey, you don't know the combination to that lock, do you, you little so-and-so?"

"Of course not!" She stamped her foot. Bob's eyes went back to the bicycle. Jennifer went on, "Probably a mouse jumped on the tire, or something."

"Don't be silly."

"The wind blew."

"Naw."

"Well, I'm leaving. I'm not just gonna *stand* here and *look* at something all the time." She stalked away.

Now Bob was alone. From a distance he could hear the putt-putt of boats in the harbor. In front of him the wheels moved around steadily, as though some spooky hand were pushing them on and on. The boy was hypnotized by what he saw.

Ordinarily, Bob was a patient fellow. He could spend a lot of time working on the tiniest little job, for his scientific interest had taught him to pay attention to details and to get things right.

*The wheels moved as though some spooky
hand were pushing them on and on.*

But this was a new experience for him: he was waiting for—what? For a wheel to stop turning? For them both to keep going? He didn't even know which he hoped for.

Bob waited, fidgeted, perspired, sat, walked back and forth, but kept his eyes on the bicycle constantly. The wheels turned and turned and turned. No faster, no slower. Time had begun to lose its meaning, when he felt a pain in his middle. Well, at least *that* makes sense, he thought. He was hungry. He hadn't had breakfast and, by noticing the shadows, he knew it was almost lunch hour. Something had to be done; he couldn't keep this vigil much longer, starving as he was.

He cleared his throat and let out a shout, "What time is it, anybody?"

His mother's voice came floating back. "Time for lunch, son! Your father'll be home any minute."

That meant it was close to twelve, Bob knew from the ferry schedule. He had come out here and spun these tires at about ten, maybe earlier. They had been moving for at least two hours, without any signs of slowing down, even yet!

Bob decided he'd have to leave the scene for food. He closed the doors quickly and ran into the house, where Jennifer was noisily slurping soup from a big spoon. She finished her lunch and ran out, while Bob ate mechanically, his mind completely occupied with the mysterious affair in the garage.

The only answer—amazing as it seemed—was that during the last two nights the bicycle wheels had continued turning (after Bob had started them) all night long—eight or ten or twelve hours—*all by themselves!*

"That," Bob told himself, "is absolutely impossible. Yet it happened, and it is happening right now. There is something about that bike— I'm going to ride her and see what *that's* like."

He ran out of the house as his mother called vainly to him to finish his milk. He crossed the driveway to the garage. The doors were open. The bike was gone! Hearing Jennifer's customary squeal, he ran out into the street. There she went, up Phinney's Lane toward town, going full tilt.

Bob settled down on a tree stump. He put his head in his hands. "Oh, no," he groaned.

Across the street he heard a voice. He looked up. There were Ingrid and Annie. One of them pointed. "She went that way."

Bob smiled weakly at the ladies and walked away.

56

6. An Interesting Passenger

Bob never did catch up with Jennifer, for a good reason: his father found him and put him to work on the ferry that very afternoon. There was so much to do that the boy forgot about the bicycle, for the time being.

For a couple of hundred years, at least, Phinney's Lane had been much like any other New England road leading from the center of town to the town dock. In the olden days, packets from Boston tied up there to load and unload, then sailed back to the city with passengers and cargo. Nowadays, fishermen set out in their dories early every weekday morning for the mussel beds. Townspeople and summer visitors kept their dinghies, sailboats, and outboards moored there.

The main part of the dock, of course, was a berth for the *Clermont,* and her principal function was to carry passengers back and forth to Sandy Neck. Sandy Neck was once a peninsula, but a capricious storm had years ago washed away the neck part of it, leaving a big, beautiful island right out in the harbor a few miles off the mainland. Even at its busiest, however, Barnstable Harbor was a small part of the broad expanse of sea, sand, rocks, and marshland that surrounded it. Sailing out toward the island, one felt swallowed up in the immensity of the sky and the ocean.

In recent times, though, the idyllic picture had changed. The United States Government had built a secret installation on the undeveloped section of Sandy Neck. The shores of the island were still populated by bathers and were still built up with summer cottages and a few snack bars. But in the center of the island, where the dunes rose and fell and where a few scraggly pines and a lot of poison ivy grew, you could now see concrete block buildings, wire fences, and uniformed guards.

It was a strange sight. People parked their cars and trailers at the town dock, along with official automobiles driven by Army sergeants. The fun-loving folk shared the cabin of the *Clermont* with men—in or out of uniform—who carried brief-cases and looked important. At Sandy Neck these men trudged inland, getting sand in their shoes, and disappeared into the concrete block buildings, while everybody else stuck to the shore and looked for a quiet spot on the lovely beach.

Just exactly what went on behind the barbed wire was supposed to be hush-hush, but it would have been impossible not to have some of the secrets leak out. Captain Fulton probably knew more about the operation than most civilians, for when the scientists and officials wanted to talk in private on the *Clermont,* they went forward on the deck and sat right under the wheelhouse where the Captain could hear every word they said. He didn't understand very much, but he had the general idea.

The government base went under the full name of the Sandy Neck Uphill Rectification Project. It was called SNURP for short. Every so often they would send a rocket shooting up into the air and it would land in the ocean a few miles out. On other occasions a man would parachute from a helicopter and come down inside the fenced area somewhere. One of the buildings was surmounted by a huge windmill that turned slowly and majestically most of the day—and most of the night too, no doubt.

Those were the SNURP activities that could be seen. As for what was hidden, Captain Fulton reported that it was amazing. He said, for instance, that the scientists were rolling big balls along a wooden platform that was higher at one end than the other. He also described an artificial waterfall where the water fell *up*. When he told this one at the table one night, his family raised their eyebrows.

"I know you think I'm loony," he smiled, "but I'm only repeatin' what I heard. Take it or leave it."

As for the purpose of SNURP, he explained it simply. They were, he revealed, trying to find out *if what goes up must come down* and, if so, *why must it come down*.

Captain Fulton had no complaints about SNURP, because it had doubled his business. There were four round trips each day, and now a head of steam was kept up all night, for sometimes he would have to make a special voyage on short notice to carry some official visitors across the water. In those cases he would have to telephone Mr. Bones, his engineer, get him out of bed, and shanghai Bob into service as deckhand.

Bob didn't object very much to working on the

Scientists were rolling big balls along
a wooden platform ...

Clermont. It was fun, and he got paid for it. Now that he was going to do it regularly, he realized that if a fellow had to work during his summer vacation, this was probably the most pleasant job available.

On the Friday in question, it was the last trip back to the mainland. Bob was coiling rope on the afterdeck as the steamship picked its way across the harbor at its cruising speed of seven knots. Now that his work was almost finished, Bob again began to think about Jennifer's bicycle and the mysterious wheels. He didn't like to have unsolved problems lying around, and he wanted to settle this one. But how? There was no one to help him.

"All hands on deck!"

It was the Captain shouting. Bob was the only hand, so he guessed the order meant that his father wanted him. He started forward. He passed the engine room and looked down to see Mr. Bones sitting there next to the two huge pistons, smoking his corncob pipe as the pistons hissed and moved up and down, turning the shaft below them. He entered the pilothouse and reported to his father.

"Son, you did me proud today," the Captain told him. "Y've got the makin's of a fine seaman." He grabbed the whistle cord and gave two blasts.

"Look at that fool, will you? Anchored right in the channel." He steered the *Clermont* close by a rowboat with three fishermen in it. One of them jumped up and shook his fist at the bigger vessel, then almost fell overboard as the wash hit his little skiff.

Bob looked in the other direction. "Dad, I think you're out of the channel. You're supposed to go to the left of that red marker, aren't you?"

His father glared at him. "Sailor, you coil the lines and I'll man the helm." He grabbed the signal and rang the bell once. Mr. Bones acknowledged and they heard him bring the engines to half ahead. "We'll just slow down as we near port," the Captain said. The ship slid along smoothly. Bob relaxed.

"Now, Bob," he went on, "what I wanted to say was, if'n you're so all-fired tangled up in this here scientific hoo-hah, you might be interested in knowin' that the big high mucky-muck from SNURP is right here aboard this ship."

Bob's eyes popped. "Narkus? Professor Sigmund Narkus? Where is he?" He looked back at the group of passengers huddled on the rear deck.

"No, son, up there." The Captain pointed to a lone figure leaning against the rail at the bow. Bob was thrilled, for Sigmund Narkus was one of the greatest scientific minds in the world. He looked closely. The Professor was real old, probably in his forties, Bob thought. The wind whipped the few straggly hairs left on his balding head. He wore torn sneakers, crumpled khaki trousers, and an old Army windbreaker. His face, neck, and the top of his head were dark from the sun.

Narkus! The genius who had helped Einstein with nuclear reactions, the brain who had exploded the myth of cosmic rays, the mastermind who was responsible for orbital flight!

Sensing his son's excitement, the Captain smiled. "Now, lad, no use getting worked up over one of them lab fellas."

"One of them lab fellas?" Bob whispered. "Are you crazy?" He quickly outlined the background and importance of Professor Narkus. "Haven't you figured it out yet, Dad? If Narkus is in charge of SNURP, and Narkus is the number one scientist we've got, then SNURP is our number one space project! I read in *Science News Letter* that they transferred him here from Cape Canaveral!"

"Really?" The Captain was impressed.

"Now, listen, Dad, you've got to tell me. Just what are they doing over there, anyway?"

"Oh, laddie," his father chuckled, "you know I

couldn't be spillin' secrets about that." He tried to look as though he knew.

Bob was quiet for a few minutes as the boat chugged shoreward. He spoke again. "You know what? I'm going to talk to him."

"Don't you dare!" his father exclaimed. "Y'll get me in hot water that way! We're all pretendin' we don't know a thing about it. You start 'em thinkin' otherwise and they'll start usin' the government launch and we'll be carryin' nothin' but kids with sandpails again. Now, lad, get back to your duties, if you don't mind. We're about to land. Got your spring lines ready?"

"Okay, Dad," Bob replied glumly.

"Besides," his father whispered, as his son was leaving the wheelhouse, "that Narkus is a terrible-tempered rascal. He never spouts a word but what it's a grouchy one. You'd be well off to steer clear of 'im, I'm tellin' you."

Bob climbed out without answering, but he made up his mind that, one way or another, he was going to meet the great Professor Narkus.

7. A Remarkable Ride

"Thank you, Bob, for doing such a good job in the garage," Mrs. Fulton remarked at breakfast.

Bob didn't reply. He was trying to finish eating before it was time to go. He barely made it. His father drained the last drop of that horrible black coffee he liked so much, stood up, and ordered, "Let's shove off!" He grabbed an orange and shoved it into his jacket pocket. "For scurvy," he explained. The two Fulton men hurried to the dock for the first sailing.

Mrs. Fulton looked at Jennifer. "Well, dear, today's the big picnic."

"That's right, Mom. Got my lunch ready?"

Mrs. Fulton nodded.

It was on the return trip of that first voyage of the day that Bob nervously made up his mind to introduce himself to Professor Narkus. He didn't know what he would say, but he would at least ask for an autograph to go with the one of John Glenn. The Professor had gone out to Sandy Neck, and now he was coming back for some reason. Bob was too busy to make an approach until after the ship was tied up at the town dock. Then he saw the thin figure of the scientist trotting down the gangplank and toward the parking lot. He climbed into an old car that was standing there.

"I can't run after him," Bob thought. The car started up with a terrible clatter and a smoking exhaust. It jerked forward into Phinney's Lane. Bob's opportunity seemed lost. But the automobile would pass right in front of the *Clermont*. Bob's brain told him no, but his feet seemed to say yes. Like hunks of lead they thumped down the gangway and out into the road. The blood was pounding in his head. He didn't know how it happened; there he was, waving at Professor Narkus, who had to bring the rickety old car to a halt or else run Bob down.

The man sat there, holding the steering wheel tightly in both hands and staring straight at Bob without saying a word or showing any emotion except what must have been extreme annoyance. After a painful pause, Bob stammered the first thing he could think of.

"Going my way, sir?"

The Professor reached over and opened the door. Bob ran around and climbed in. Now he was committed. He had an hour before the *Clermont* sailed again. He hoped he could get back in time. The Professor fiddled with the gear shift of the old Model A Ford he was driving and finally got the conveyance moving again. They jerked and smoked up Phinney's Lane. Bob was wondering what to do next, when the man spoke.

"Adonde va?"

"Pardon me, sir?" Bob asked.

"Dove vai? Wo gehen Sie? Where you going?"

It was then that Bob discovered that Professor Narkus, who was reputed to know many languages, used them all at once. Fortunately, English was included. Bob turned and looked at the man's blue eyes, shaggy brows, and big nose. There were interesting lines in his face, and Bob felt that he was staring into the face of a genius, all right. The man asked again, and Bob tried to think of an answer.

"Craigville Beach," he blurted out, recalling Jennifer's picnic plans. "I'm looking for my sister. She's with the Brownies."

"*Ding how,*" the scientist said in Chinese. He drove on wordlessly. They went through Main Street in Barnstable. Then Bob got his courage up.

"Professor Narkus——" he began.

The man jerked his head in Bob's direction and barked, "Ho, *vous savez* my name!"

"Yes, sir, everybody knows who you are."

The Narkus skin turned from brown to red. "Trouble with you local *paisanos,* you butt into our business! *Écoutez bien*, my friend, forget who I am." He went back to driving, and Bob felt very uncomfortable. Grouchy, just like his father said.

They circled the big rotary at the Mid-Cape Highway, and the Professor slanted the car onto the winding, hilly shortcut to Craigville. In a few moments they came upon a gang of girls in Brownie uniforms. Each girl was pushing her bike up the sharp incline.

"*Mahinda rappo lapoozi?*" the Professor asked in an obscure Zulu dialect. "Your sister there?" He slowed down. Bob couldn't see Jennifer so he shook his head, and the Professor stepped on the gas again to get moving. Halfway up the grade they looked ahead and saw a lone figure on a bicycle proceeding uphill ahead of them. It was Jennifer. She was pedaling gaily as though she were on the flat. The Model A passed

"Ding How," the scientist said in Chinese.

her as Bob pointed and told the Professor who it was.

"Get out at the top," he grunted. Reaching the summit, he pulled over. Bob jumped out, pretending that he wanted his sister to stop, though he didn't know what he would say if she did. But he had to go along with the ruse. Luckily, Jennifer whizzed by with a happy cry.

Professor Narkus raised his eyebrows. "Like the Orient Express she pedals," he said with some puzzlement. *"Pronto!"* he ordered Bob. "Get in. We catch her."

The boy leaped in and they took off with a rattle, down the other side of what was known as Shootflying Hill. But Jennifer was way ahead of them. By the time the automobile was up to full speed, they knew they could not catch her.

"Vierzig kilometren," the driver shouted in amazement, as he looked at the speedometer, "and she beats us!" He gripped the wheel as he guided the rattletrap vehicle down the grade at the dizzying speed. They reached the bottom and leveled off. A moment later they saw Jennifer standing at the side of the highway, apparently waiting for them.

"Fatihah!" the Professor cried in Arabic. "I cannot stop! I go too fast!" He pressed his foot

against the brake, but it didn't have much effect. The speeding automobile then started up Clay Hill, the next steep climb on the way to Craigville Beach. Bob looked back.

"She's coming after us!" he yelled.

Professor Narkus pressed his foot on the gas. *"Erin go bragh!"* he cried. "It is my intention to park in the middle of the road when we get to the top and block the way!"

Bob looked back. "She's catching up!" he said.

It was true. Remarkably, Jennifer Fulton pumped her bike up Clay Hill so fast that she caught up with the Ford and passed it. She was helped, of course, by the fact that the car slowed in its climb. Nevertheless, it was a most unusual feat, and for once the great scientist showed more interest than annoyance. As the auto chugged to the highest point on Clay Hill, the Professor pulled over to the side and stopped. Jennifer rapidly disappeared in the distance.

Bob watched the scientist's face, and knew he was doing some heavy thinking. The lips twitched, the jaw muscles tightened, and the eyes blinked and stared. Bob also knew that the behavior of the bicycle had aroused the man's curiosity. It had some connection with the unexplained ever-turning wheels, Bob was sure. But he was not ready to risk the Narkus temper by intruding any of his own theories right now. So he kept silent.

"*Quid hoc sibi vult?*" the man suddenly burst out. "What does this mean? Does your sister's vehicle have a motor?"

"No. It has no motor in it at all."

Professor Narkus shook his head from side to side. "I was shifting into second and going twenty kilometers. She passed me. A most peculiar affair. Seems to violate all the laws of physics, *n'est-ce pas?*"

"Yes."

The Professor looked sharply at Bob. "Oh, you know something about physics, do you? Pardon me, young man, I never did hear your name."

"Robert Fulton, sir."

"Ah, yes, the son of *El Capitán* Fulton. I have heard him speak of you. Well, what do *you* think of this business?" He poked a finger in the direction Jennifer had taken.

"Well, Professor," Bob declared, "I do have a theory."

"*Kharasho*. Let's hear it."

Starting from the beginning, Bob described the whole series of events of recent days: the Pop Stretcher explosion, the damaged Sussex Speedster, his repair work on it, and the mystery of the moving wheels.

"I never did get a chance to test the bike myself," Bob concluded, "because I had to go to work on the ferryboat. But I feel sure there is something worth investigating there."

The Professor, who had listened intently to Bob's story, sat up with a jerk, turned the key, and got the engine going. "You feel right, young man. Let's take a look at that bike. *Andiamo!*"

About five minutes later he steered the Model A into the Craigville Beach parking lot. Bob and the Professor leaped out and searched for the Brownies. It was an easy search, for all they had to do was find the source of the screeching and howling of twenty-five girls. The Brownies were in the picnic area under the pine trees. The men waded through the mob until they found Jennifer at last.

"Where's your bike?" Bob asked her. She pointed. He ran over to a pile of two-wheelers lying on the ground and picked out the Sussex Speedster. The Professor grabbed it and gave it a thorough inspection. He spun the pedals and the wheels. He moved the handlebars, smelled the chain, and ran his forefinger over the bearings. All the while he grunted to himself. Bob watched him. Finally the man set the bike down and straightened up.

He gave it a thorough inspection.

"Now, Robert—you don't mind if I call you Robert, do you?"

"Oh, no, sir."

"I want to inspect this bicycle more carefully, Robert. Do you think it would be possible for you to bring it over to my laboratory at Sandy Neck as soon as you can? This just might have some bearing on our experiments there."

"I think so, Professor, if Jennifer'll let it go."

"Good. Do that, then. And another thing, *bitte*, do not let anyone know what we have seen here today. Now, come on, you've got to get back to work, and I'm too late for the appointment I had."

The two of them got into the car and began the noisy ride back to Phinney's Lane. Neither spoke. The Professor was probably solving formulas in his head. Bob, of course, was pinching himself to make sure it wasn't a dream: he and Professor Narkus sharing an important secret together.

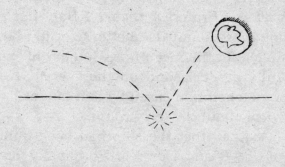

8. A Scientific Break-through

For years afterward Bob claimed that the most difficult time of the whole exciting summer was trying to explain to Jennifer why her bicycle had to be taken away. He finally was forced to tell her the entire story—that the action of the wheels was going to be analyzed by the SNURP scientists in connection with their work.

"And don't forget, this is a secret!" he warned. "And that means don't tell anyone!"

Jennifer's eyes widened as she moved her head slowly and emphatically from side to side. "Oh, no. I won't tell a soul. Honest. You know me, Bob."

"Yes, I know you. That's why I said it."

So, on one of his trips across the harbor, Bob delivered the Sussex Speedster to the gates of the SNURP compound. The next time he took the boat the Professor thanked Bob, but said . nothing more about the matter. Nor did he for eight days. In the meantime, Bob did his work faithfully as deckhand on the *Clermont*. His father watched him carefully and taught him a good deal about the ferry routine.

Bob learned that the ship had been built in 1892 at City Island, New York, originally for use as a police launch in New York harbor. She was then rebuilt some years later as a pleasure yacht. When her owner went broke in the 1930s, the town of Barnstable purchased her. The *Clermont* was twenty-one gross tons, beautifully constructed with yellow pine planking and oak frames and keel. She was sixty-four feet in length, eleven in the beam, and drew four feet of water. Her original speed was a respectable fourteen knots, but her boiler was not what it used to be, and it was limited by law to 125 pounds, a condition which confined the vessel to seven knots.

On the ninth day after he had handed over the bicycle, Bob threw a line to the Sandy Neck landing on the first trip of the day and saw the Profes-

*Bob did his work faithfully
as a deckhand . . .*

sor standing there with the bike. He pushed it up the gangplank.

Bob asked eagerly, "What did you find out?"

The scientist's face remained grim as he answered, in Hindustani, "*Sabr karo*, Bob. Have patience. When we reach the mainland, we'll meet in your garage and I shall explain as much as I can. Bring your father."

Despite the suggestion, Bob was not very patient, yet there was nothing he could do except wait. Eventually, however, the three of them were gathered in the garage, where Bob and Captain Fulton waited rather nervously while Professor Narkus filled his pipe. He puffed a few times and finally spoke.

"Robert, you made one fine discovery when you fixed *cet vélocipède*. That bicycle has bearings without friction. You know what that means, gentlemen? That means we're on the track of something big like—like—well, like splitting the atom."

The Professor fell silent, as if to let the message sink in. The other two looked more puzzled than excited.

Bob finally said, "I'm not sure I follow you, Professor. Why would that bike be any different?"

"Well, from listening to your description of the

incident, my conclusion is that when the Pop Stretcher blew up, it forced the product of the explosion into the wheels, pedals, gears, and vital parts of the bike. And that sticky stuff is like a magic formula—it stops friction, so the wheels keep turning. A little baby could move them." The Professor's pipe went out.

Bob scratched his head. "I thought I cleaned all that stuff off the bike."

"But you didn't clean way inside the little bearings and gears." The scientist lit his pipe again. He puffed words and smoke together. "That's—where—the—friction—comes from."

Bob thought a moment. Then he exclaimed, "Gee, if that stuff eliminates friction, that means there isn't anything to hold the bike back. I see what you mean by a fine discovery. If you applied it to automobiles, trains, rocket engines, airplanes—why it would save so much power it would revolutionize the whole transportation industry!"

"Exactement."

"What in the name of Neptune are you two blabbing about?" Captain Fulton suddenly blurted out.

"Well, Dad—may I explain it, Professor?" The scientist nodded. Bob went on. "Take Jennifer's bicycle—or take any vehicle. When you try to

81

make it go, there are two things that hold it back. One is air resistance and the other is friction resistance."

"I know about air, m'boy," the Captain eagerly burst out. "When the huge mains'l bellies out, and the trade winds slant across your stern, and your bow plunges into the surf, y'know what she's—"

"Yes, yes, Dad, that's right," Bob interrupted. "But friction is the phenomenon we're concerned with here. Now look!"

He took a silver coin from his pocket, placed it on the planking at one end of the workbench, and snapped it with his finger. The coin skidded a couple of feet and then stopped.

"Why did it come to a stop, Dad? Friction." Bob answered his own question.

The boy then bent over to Jennifer's bicycle, which was lying on its side. He gently poked at the front wheel and it moved. "Why won't this wheel stop, Dad? *No* friction! With friction eliminated at the wheel bearings, there is only air resistance to make any difference."

"What about air, then?" asked the Captain.

"Inside the garage, it wouldn't have much effect on the situation, and that's why the wheels turned all night. Outdoors, of course, when you're *riding* the bike, it slows you down, but not much. In faster-moving objects, air resistance can be considerable. You see, it increases as— as—"

"As the square of the speed," the Professor chimed in, as Bob hesitated. "*Exempli gratia:* at sixty miles per hour, it is four times as great as at thirty."

"But even at top speeds," Bob said, "air resistance is no more than two thirds of the total resistance to motion. At lower speeds, it is friction that does most of the dirty work. That's why Jennifer was whizzing around here like a speed demon. She barely had to pump to keep going."

"Well, blow me down," whispered Captain Fulton in awe.

"And speak of the devil!" Professor Narkus exclaimed, as the garage doors were pulled open and Jennifer's slight figure came into view.

"Say," she cried, "how about my bike! Can I have it now? Can I?"

"Sure, honey," said the scientist, "and you're a *bella ragazza* for letting me keep it all this time. I'll pay you back somehow. *Spasebo.*"

The girl pounced on the two-wheeler with joy and was gone in a wink. Professor Narkus closed the doors, shutting the group in the garage again. He knocked the ashes from his pipe, looked up, and spoke in most somber tones.

"Can I have it? Can I have it now?"

"Gentlemen, I have something of extreme importance to reveal now. Bob's discovery of frictionless bearings appears to solve one of the great unsolvables. Like perpetual motion, it was thought that eliminating friction was impossible, for it would contradict the laws of nature. But with this new development, we can see new horizons opened up to us. And particularly in connection with our work at Sandy Neck."

"Do you mean you're working on friction there?" Bob asked.

"Bob, and *Señor Capitán*," the scientist said seriously, "I am now going to have to reveal top-secret information, because I want your cooperation. No need for me to tell you about security regulations and all that, is there?"

The others shook their heads.

"The Sandy Neck Uphill Rectification Project is a fancy name for antigravity research. We have reason to believe that gravitation is growing weaker, that it varies not only according to where on the earth it is measured, but also according to how long it is applied. I can't make it all clear to you now, but just remember that Newton found that gravity varies inversely according to the square of the distance between the two masses, and—oh, you know all that."

"Aye, of course we do," the Captain assured him.

"Now, we have had some success in slowing down the acceleration of gravity between two bodies. You can imagine the implications in reference to space exploration."

Bob's jaw dropped, for he truly did see the picture.

"And," Professor Narkus concluded, "with our friction problems now out of the way—why, the mind reels. *Incroyable!*" He slapped his forehead with his palm, hardly able to believe it himself. The men were all silent for a few moments. Bob thought he heard a noise at the door, but aside from that there was just the heavy breathing of the older men to break the stillness.

Finally the Professor spoke again. "Now, Robert, what do you call that magic stuff that you put in the Pop Stretcher?"

"Why, just Zeta. Ingredient Zeta."

"*Ach,* that's a good mysterious name all right," chuckled the scientist. "Now, just turn over to me, for the government, all the Zeta you have left. We'll analyze it and start producing it. There really isn't enough in the works of Jennifer's bicycle for our men to do anything with."

Bob spread out his palms. "But there isn't any

Zeta left. It was all destroyed in the explosion."

"Oh, *rhy ddrwg!*" the man said in Welsh. "Too bad. Well, the next best thing. Give me the formula."

"Gosh, I don't have it written down. I made a whole batch a couple of weeks ago——"

"You don't have it written down!" The Professor seemed to jump a foot off the ground. His pipe wiggled in his mouth and finally fell right out of it. His face got red, and the Fultons were witness to an exhibition of the famous Narkus grouch. "What kind of a *scientifico* are you? Then what is it? Tell it to me quick!" He pulled a pad and pencil out of his pocket.

Bob squirmed. "Gee, I don't really *remember* it exactly. I'd have to sit down and think——"

The scientist slapped the book shut and put it away. He glared.

"All right, if that's your attitude. Now, I shall return to my offices to study what data we now have on this matter. In the meantime, I suggest you do just that—sit down and think—and you had better come up with something for us about this Zeta, or we'll be mighty suspicious of your motives, Robert Fulton. Come, Captain, it's time for the ferry." He barged out of the garage.

Captain Fulton paused a moment, and said

"*What kind of scientifico are you?*"

sympathetically to his son, "Forget about the *Clermont*, lad, until you've nailed this down." He walked after the scientist.

Bob slumped down onto a stool, wondering just *what* exactly he had mixed into Ingredient Zeta.

9. A Helpful Discovery

Bob spent several hours racking his brain for the vital information Professor Narkus wanted so badly. His first move was to grab a pencil stub from the grimy worktable and write down all he could remember on the pad of yellow paper he used for notes and stuff. He crossed out part of the list and added more.

The tough part was to recall not only *what* had gone into the mixture but *how much*. A couple of times Bob ran into the kitchen and studied the contents of the shelves and the vegetable bin. He also thumbed through the *Raspberry Hill Cook Book*, a volume which had helped him immeasurably in the past in the chemical offshoots of his experiments.

When his mother heard what he was doing, she kept on shelling peas but called sarcastically, "Don't forget the fifty pounds of sugar!" Her head waggled from side to side in disbelief.

After a quick lunch Bob was back outside, leaning his elbows on the worn but smooth wood of the bench, staring out of the filthy window at the outline of Sandy Neck in the distance.

"Hello, Bobby," cracked a voice, directly behind him.

"How are you?" cackled another.

The startled boy nearly jumped right out of his skin. He turned and made out two dumpy figures standing inside the garage. As his vision focused in the gloom, he saw they were Ingrid and Annie, the knitting neighbors from across the lane. They stood there smiling, each holding in one hand a huge cloth bag with numerous pointed and colored needles sticking out the top or through the bottom. Loops of yarn hung down and trailed away out of sight in the distance.

Bob recovered from his surprise. "Hello, Miss Ingrid. Hello, Miss Annie." He was polite, especially as in the two years since they moved in he had never learned which of the ladies was which, nor even what their last names were. "Now, what in the world are they hanging around here for?" he asked himself.

"We wondered about that terrible explosion," one of them said. "Hoped you weren't hurt."

"So this is your laboratory," said the other, peering into one corner and then another.

"It *was*," Bob replied, and he explained how he was going to have to work on the ferryboat the rest of the summer.

"Oh, what a shame," murmured Ingrid—or was it Annie? "Then you won't invent any more."

"And you won't have to lock the doors any more," added Annie or was it Ingrid?

Bob squinted at these strange people. How did they seem to know so much? Of course, they sat on the porch all day, and they could see right across the street, and probably hear all that was said. Ingrid and Annie shuffled forward a little more. They wore old bedroom slippers, knee-high socks, faded print dresses with pins at the throat, and their hair was straggly and pointed in all directions. Then Bob noticed knitting needles in their hair too, sticking out like extra-long hatpins—but no hats. He shivered a tiny bit. Was he afraid of these funny-looking old ladies?

"That is interesting, isn't it? About the bicycle and the turning wheels," one of them remarked.

Was he afraid of these funny-looking old ladies?

"Those gentlemen at Sandy Neck must be fascinated by it," the other added.

Bob shivered again. "You—you *know?*"

"Oh, my, yes," came the reply. "Jennifer told us everything."

"Why, she even let us have a ride on the famous bike!" exulted the other knitter. They both giggled.

Bob took a deep, deep breath and sighed. Imagine the United States Government expecting Jennifer Fulton to keep a secret! As he stood there, looking disgustedly at the two women, there was a sudden commotion outside, and a group of boys and girls—friends of Jennifer's— appeared at the door.

"Hey, Bob," one of them cried, "fix our bikes, will ya?"

There was activity as the knot of youngsters pushed their two-wheelers inside the garage. Ingrid and Annie backed up against the side, and the space filled with shouting children.

"We want to ride fast, like Jenny," one of the girls piped up.

"Yeah," said a boy. "We want them friendless borings."

Frictionless bearings! How did *they* know? The Professor had told the story only this morning, Bob realized. Exasperated, he waved his arm around the garage.

"Look, kids, this place was wrecked when the Pop Stretcher exploded. I don't have the tools or the——" He stopped talking and froze. He stared past Ingrid and Annie, who had taken out their knitting and were leaning against the work-bench, clicking and clacking their needles. Behind them, in a dark corner, was the vague shape of the trash barrel. In it, Bob suddenly remembered, were rags soaked with the residue from the blowup, as well as the sticky remains of several cheesecloth bags filled with Zeta that had been destroyed in the catastrophe.

"Why, gosh!" he told himself. "There must be quite a bit of the vital stuff right there in that barrel." He rushed over and looked. He couldn't see a thing. Too dark. "Gimme the flashlight!" he said, to nobody in particular, as he ran and grabbed it from a shelf. He pressed the button and illuminated the inside of the big bin. His heart leaped. Full of it! Filled with rags and bags, and on the bottom at least several inches of gunk that seemed to contain slices of roots, rinds, and what-not! It was a tremendous supply of Ingredient Zeta—tremendous compared to what had existed before this discovery.

"Say," he announced out loud, "there's enough Zeta here for the SNURP scientists to analyze till they're blue in the face."

Ingrid and Annie grinned broadly. One of them click-clacked her needles as her eyes concentrated on Bob's list of ingredients.

"What's this, Bobby?" she asked. "Making a spring tonic?"

The other woman asked, "Zeta? What's that?"

Then the kids started howling again. "Come on, Bob, fix our bikes, fix our bikes!"

Bob wanted to yell back and tell everyone to clear out. But he decided the easiest way to get rid of them was to give in. "All right, leave them and wait outside!" He pushed the little gang out and shut the doors. He seized a rag from the barrel and quickly applied enough of the goo on the axles of the bikes so that the wheels spun easily. It took only a few minutes, and then he let the youngsters back in. They jumped on their vehicles and scooted up the lane and out of sight, shouting and challenging each other to races.

Bob watched them go, stood daydreaming for a moment, then turned back to the garage. Now, to tell Professor Narkus about the extra supply of Zeta, and to fill him in on the formula as he remembered it. Bob hurried to the workbench and was brought up short when he realized that the two knitters were still with him.

"Well, ladies, I must leave now. Thank you for dropping by."

Ingrid or Annie thrust the pad of yellow paper forward. "Is this what you're looking for, Bobby?" He took it from her.

Annie or Ingrid said, "Don't forget to lock up, now." The two strange women waddled out, down the driveway and across the lane to their home. Bob had to grin as he watched them leave. "Some characters!" he thought. He tore off the page with the formula and threw the pad down on the bench. He rushed into the house and called SNURP on the telephone. In a few seconds he had been put through to Professor Narkus and he heard the familiar voice.

"*Pronto!*"

"Professor, it's me, Bob." He described what he had found in the garage.

"Excellent, son. How about the formula: have you written that down, too?"

Bob held the yellow paper in his hand. "Got it right here, sir."

"*Muy bien, amigo.* Now, hop on the first ferry and get over here. I'll see that they let you in at the gate."

Bob hung up, looked at his watch, and saw that he could catch the first afternoon boat if he wasted no time. He ran down the back steps and almost knocked his mother over. She was coming home from some shopping.

"Oh, Bob," she said, "would you take the groceries out of the car, please?"

"Gee, Mom, I *can't!* I've got to get over to the Professor's office right now. There just isn't time." The *Clermont*'s whistle blasted. She was about to leave.

"All right," his mother said, waving her hand. "Go ahead."

The boy ran down the road to the dock and jumped aboard the boat's stern as it pulled away. At that moment he remembered he had failed to lock the garage.

10. An Assignment for Bob

On the way to Sandy Neck, Bob told his father the latest development. The Captain nodded with interest. As the two parted, when the boat reached the island, the father said slyly, "Don't forget about the swimmin' exhibition you promised us."

"What?"

"Your own words: 'If fixin' the bike leads to anything,' ye vowed, 'I'll swim to Sandy Neck under water.' Wouldn't y'say, it's led to somethin'?" He put his head back and roared with laughter. Bob went down the gangplank thinking, "As if I didn't have enough to worry about."

He trudged through the dunes and presented

*The windmill was driven by an arrangement
of weights and pulleys . . .*

himself at the heavily guarded entrance to SNURP and was admitted after being identified. Some distance away he could see the Professor, standing at the door of the main building waiting for him. Bob walked over, and the two greeted each other.

"Come, Bob, I'll show you around a little bit before we meet the staff."

The scientist then pointed out a few fascinating features of the Sandy Neck Uphill Rectification Project. The windmill that everybody could see from the mainland was not driven by the wind, Bob was surprised to learn, but by an ingenious arrangement of cables, weights, and pulleys underneath it. This, in turn, was activated by changes in barometric pressure. It was most unusual.

Inside the main laboratory, the Professor showed Bob how bowling balls were made to move up an incline. The whole experiment was enclosed in a vacuum, and strange-looking tubes moved back and forth along the sides of the runway. The black spheres moved up and down with them.

"These bowling balls are hollow, Bob," the man revealed. "Some day we'll use real ones, I hope, and your Ingredient Zeta is going to help a lot. *Allakazam!* Look at the time! We've got to get to our meeting. Come on."

The scientist led the boy through the cool, well-lighted corridors of the simple, unadorned building. They came to some double doors and entered. They were in a large conference room, furnished with a long table surrounded by chairs, and that was about all. Standing around in two or three little groups were quite a few men in uniform. Bob could see from the insignia that they were mostly generals. One of them spoke.

"Ah, here we are. And this is the boy Fulton, I presume?"

Professor Narkus introduced Bob. "This is General Gates, Bob, project head at SNURP."

"All right, men," ordered General Gates, "let's see what we have here. Be seated, please."

Bob quickly learned that the meeting was a briefing session for the military staff at SNURP. Professor Narkus took up most of the time himself, reading from his notes or scribbling on the blackboard. He told the whole story of the Pop Stretcher, the explosion, the frictionless bearings, Zeta and its significance. The officers listened intently, for it was an amazing yarn, Bob realized, as he heard it all spelled out so thoroughly and well by the scientist.

When he had finished, there was a long silence.

*"All right, men. Let's see what
we have here . . ."*

General Gates broke it. "Remarkable," he said. "And you believe, Professor, that this Zeta can aid us in our antigravity research?"

"I am convinced of it."

"All right. Now, young man, just what is in it?"

Bob fidgeted. "Well, sir, I am not sure, but I have made up this recipe from memory." He held out the yellow paper.

"Not sure!" the General echoed. He grabbed the paper with one hand and put on his spectacles with the other. "Let's see this." He started reading. "Lemon rinds, cornstarch, sodium chloride, soybean oil, ginger, peppercorns, sassafras root, yeast. Great Scott—this sounds like sweet-and-sour pork sauce! What are you trying to do, boy, make donkeys out of the Sandy Neck Uphill Rectification Project? Do you really expect us to believe this is the secret formula, the Zeta that Narkus declares is so valuable?"

"Don't forget, General," the Professor answered sharply, "this started out as a method of making soda pop."

"Hmmm, yes," the officer mumbled, staring at the paper. "Well, what do we do next?"

The Professor then explained that the exact formula of Zeta was not known, but that Bob's recollection of it—plus the supply that had been

104

found in the Fulton garage—would almost certainly make it possible to determine precisely what went into the substance.

"However," he added, *"yog-yog karump glooby bosh, karump o'flibber."*

The General shifted impatiently in his chair. "Just what in the world are you talking about?"

"It's an old saying that the Australian Bushmen are very fond of. Loosely translated, it means: 'He who takes last step first walks backwards.'" The Professor stuck an index finger toward the ceiling for emphasis. "It applies here, because we have neglected to mention one important matter. It was *not* the Zeta the boy put into the machine that eliminated friction. It was the distillation of it—plus some other ingredients such as water, sugar, and Coke—*inside* the Pop Stretcher. If it hadn't exploded, we never would have made the discovery. Therefore, we have to re-create the process; we must construct another Pop Stretcher to obtain Zeta-plus!"

Bob's eyes widened. He admitted to himself that even he had not fully recognized this.

The General remarked dryly, "I hope we don't have to blow one up each time we want some Zeta, or whatever it is."

The Professor didn't think that would be

necessary; he thought that the distillation process alone would produce the desired material for eliminating friction.

"All right, Professor, you've got your green light," the General said, "but I hope it doesn't have to go by the name of 'Pop Stretcher.' When they hear that in Washington, they'll never let us spend the money. And heaven help us if the thing doesn't work when we get it finished!"

The Professor shrugged his shoulders, not knowing what to suggest.

"Sir, I've got an idea," one of the other officers said to the General. "We can call it a Crash Program. They always understand that kind of language down there."

"Excellent, Major!" The General stood up, bade good-by to Bob and the Professor as he handed back the paper with Bob's formula on it, and trooped out with all his men.

The Professor clapped Bob on the shoulder. "Good news! Now, sit down here a moment while I tell you what you have to do."

He explained that Bob would merely have to build a scale model of his original Pop Stretcher, from which the SNURP scientists would erect a full-sized machine, capable of manufacturing enough Zeta-plus—as he now called the stuff that Bob had once thought was mere evil-smelling goo—to supply the needs of the government experiments.

"But, Professor, that'll take a lot of equipment I don't have any more," Bob protested.

"We'll supply everything. You just make out a list of what you need. Do it *precipitando*, so we waste no time. And make sure you get it right!"

Bob took a pencil and paper from the conference table and began writing down his requirements. He conferred with Professor Narkus on some items, and after a half hour he had finished. The Professor looked at the final list.

"Oh, I think we can have these things sent over to your place tomorrow sometime. Come, I'll walk to the ferry with you."

Just before Bob said farewell to his friend at the gangplank, the Professor seemed to think of something.

"Say, Bob," he said brightly, "I meant to show you this." He pulled at a gold chain, and out of his pocket came a lovely old Hamilton watch. "I must confess. Last week when I had the bike, I scraped a little of Zeta-plus off the axle with a toothpick and I applied it to the balance wheel bearings and the movement of this watch. Look, it goes perfectly, and I haven't wound it for seven

"I haven't wound it for seven days."

days. Now you see why I compared your discovery with splitting the atom. Think of all that this means, my boy!"

Bob began to feel the pressure. He well understood the importance of the task he had been given, but he had no way of knowing whether he could deliver. He hadn't remembered the formula, and now he was not sure he could remember the details of his original Pop Stretcher.

"But, Professor," he squinted into the sun as he looked at his acquaintance, "what if you build the big Pop Stretcher and—and it doesn't manufacture the correct substance?"

The scientist's eyes flashed and his face reddened. He barked, "It better had, that's all!" He marched away. Bob boarded the ferry with a lump in his throat.

11. Dirty Work on Phinney's Lane

"Another scone, Ingrid?" Mrs. Fulton was asking. They sat in the parlor of the Fulton home having tea at about the same time that Bob was consulting with the generals.

The woman shook her head and smiled, as she continued knitting.

"Where's your friend?" Mrs. Fulton asked.

"Annie? Oh, she's probably home canning. She is putting up jars of things for the Arawaks."

"The Arawaks? Are those the poor, starving Indian creatures in the Caribbean that you and Annie are always sending clothes to?"

"Yes," Ingrid smiled. "We just sent a package

off the other day, and we shall no doubt get something in the mail tomorrow."

"My, that is wonderful. You know, I should be doing something like that, but I just don't seem to have the time," Mrs. Fulton sighed.

Long after the scones and the tea were gone, the two ladies sat and chatted. Finally they were interrupted when Mrs. Fulton's son came charging up the steps and into the house. He slammed the door, as usual.

"Robert"—he gritted his teeth when she used that name—"you remember Miss—Miss Ingrid, don't you?"

Bob nodded and smiled.

"Where have you been, son?" his mother called as he went on out of the room.

"Oh—Sandy Neck," he answered carelessly. "Gotta build a model of the Pop Str——" He bit his lip as he ran upstairs to his room. He remembered he was now subject to government security regulations. "Must keep my big mouth shut," he said to himself.

But Ingrid's alert ears had picked up enough. Her knitting needles clicked and clacked for a few minutes, and then she stuffed her things into her big bag and stood up.

"Thank you so much, Mrs. Fulton, but I must be going."

"Do come again, Ingrid, now that you know where we are."

The women said good-by at the front door, and Ingrid shuffled across the lane and into her own home. Annie greeted her with a toothy smile. "You kept her busy."

"Did you get the stuff?" Ingrid asked hoarsely.

"Did I get the stuff? Look!" Annie took her friend by the arm and pulled her into the kitchen. There on the table was the pail, containing some black liquid. The two women practically drooled.

"Ingredient Zeta!" whispered Ingrid in awe. "This will put our country ahead of both the United States and the Russians! She seized her friend's hands in her own. "And have I something for you!" She repeated what Bob had told his mother.

Annie's face was flushed with excitement. "Ingrid Fundamento, you are a sly one! Not only a sample of Zeta, but maybe a crack at the Pop Stretcher. Maybe we'll get a promotion out of this."

"That's enough daydreaming, dear. Let's get these things ready to go."

Ingrid and Annie busied themselves preparing packages. When finished, they had one neat parcel containing some of the fancy knitted goods they made so skillfully. The other contained a jam jar labeled "Preserves," and the contents of the jar were really yummy-looking. Pieces of cardboard were arranged to prevent breakage during shipping.

When they were ready, the women tucked the boxes under their arms, left the house, and shuffled up Phinney's Lane to Main Street. There they turned right and got to the Post Office just before five, when it closed.

"Parcel post to Tierra Ninguno," they told the clerk.

"Ah, ladies," he purred, "more good works for the Arawaks, eh?"

They nodded pleasantly, and the man looked at their customs declaration. "Just a formality," he smiled. He weighed and stamped the packages, accepted the ladies' money, and gave them their change. They started shuffling home.

"Too bad you couldn't get more of the stuff," Annie whispered as they went down Phinney's Lane.

"It doesn't matter. One jar is enough to give an idea."

"I guess you're right, Ingrid, as usual."

"And when the kid finishes that Pop Stretcher, we will have to work fast."

113

"We must keep the place under constant observation."

They shuffled on toward home and, as they reached their walk, they spied the quaint figure of Captain Fulton stomping up from the town dock. The ladies halted. He saw them and bowed with a flourish.

"Ah, two lovely specimens of womankind, if ever I seen 'em, and I've seen 'em in many a port from here to Cathay!" he declared, to the amusement of the women.

"Oh, Captain, you shouldn't," giggled Annie. Ingrid blushed.

The Captain held up his hand. "Tut, tut. I mean every word of it. And if ever you feel the need of a little cruise to cure the vapors, just say th' word and the *Clermont* is at your service—on the house, as the landlubbers put it."

"Oh, thank you, sir," Ingrid gushed. "We'd love to ride to Sandy Neck some moonlit night. Could we?"

"Your wish is my command. When ready, name the date." He bowed handsomely again and thumped into his house. The knitters shuffled into theirs, where Annie congratulated her friend.

"Oh, you're a sly one, Ingrid Fundamento."

"The handsome fool," Ingrid muttered with contempt. "That crazy ferryboat of his is going to come in very handy one of these days. You'll see."

12. An Unanswered Question

A day or two later the supplies arrived and Bob got started on his model Pop Stretcher. Here again, he was operating from memory. He had a difficult time reconstructing in his mind the contraption as he remembered it before it had destroyed itself. Even more troublesome was the requirement that it be a scale model, small enough so that it could be transported easily from place to place, and yet accurate enough so the SNURP scientists could make a perfect, workable large Pop Stretcher from it.

Once more the garage had been turned into a laboratory. There was no room for an automobile. Jennifer now kept her bicycle in her bedroom, anyway, when she could get away with it, because she liked it so much. Captain Fulton had to hire another high school boy to crew aboard the *Clermont*, for he knew Bob was going to be tied up for a long time to come.

"Besides," he said to his wife, switching his ground completely, "that boy's got the makin's of an Albert Einstein, if'n I ever seen one. He's got to experiment and experiment, you know. How's he ever going to find out anything if'n he don't experiment?"

"You're so right, dear."

At that very moment Bob was practically knee-deep in drawings that he had made and discarded. He was using Jennifer's scribble paper because he couldn't find his favorite pad of yellow foolscap, and he was trying to outline the basic components of his original Pop Stretcher. He couldn't seem to get it right, but each sketch was closer to the truth and he knew he'd hit it eventually.

He was still doing this in the late afternoon of that day when the Professor appeared at the door of the garage-laboratory. With him was an assistant carrying a large container for chemicals. The Professor mopped his brow.

"We'd have been here sooner," he said in disgust, "but that doggone *kaipuke* of your father's

Bob was practically knee-deep
in drawings ...

ran aground. We were marooned for hours waiting for the tide to come in. Now, where are the leftovers?"

"Here." Bob led them to the trash barrel.

"Ka pai," the Professor answered, using the Maori tongue again. He tipped the container to see better. "There isn't as much as I had thought, from your description, Robert."

Bob looked inside, lighting it with the flashlight. To his dismay he noticed that where there had been quite a supply, now there wasn't.

"Why, this stuff must be subject to evaporation. The other day there was a lot of the residue. Now it's just a film on the bottom."

"Cela ne fait rien. No matter. We'll do the best we can by extracting the juice from these rags and bags here. Andrew, will you pack this up?" The assistant began transferring the things from the bin to the container he had brought with him. He finished shortly, and the two men hurried out to catch the ferry, which was way off schedule now because of its grounding.

Bob tried to go on with his task, but he couldn't concentrate, wondering about the Zeta in the barrel. He mechanically put his things away, locked up the lab, and went in to get ready for supper. He washed up and then sat on his bed to think. He was still thinking when he was called to

119

the table, and he hadn't come to any conclusion at all.

"Well, Bob," Captain Fulton said as he bit into his whale steak, "what's the scuttlebutt on frictionless bearings?"

Bob looked up. "Gee, Dad, that's top-secret stuff you're talking about."

"Now, Robert," Mrs. Fulton began. He darted a look at her. "Bob, I should say—it's all right to discuss something that we all know about. Really, everybody must know. Why, only the other day Annie—or was it Ingrid—was right here in this house chatting with me about the whole affair."

"I wouldn't believe anything *they* said," Jennifer piped up.

"But, Mom," Bob protested, "that's the idea of security; so that the word won't get spread around so much that even spies finally hear about what we are doing."

"Now, *really!*" Mrs. Fulton declared. "You're not going to tell me those old ladies are *spies!*"

"They're liars, not spies," Jennifer interjected.

"Jennifer!" her mother said sharply. "You are not to use that language about anybody, much less our neighbors."

"Well, they are," the girl said, tears coming to

her eyes. "They've ruined my social studies report that I have to have on the first day of school."

"Now, miss, just what is this all about, pray tell?" the Captain queried.

"Well," she was blubbering a little, but they could still understand her, "Ingrid and Annie gave me some cookies if I'd let them ride my bike. So I did, and then they said they had to make a package for the Indians. The Indians were starving and going around without any clothes they were so poor." She blubbered, and her mother had to dry her daughter's eyes.

"You mean the Arawak tribe?" someone asked.

Jennifer cried out, "That's it! They spelled it for me and I even wrote it down. The teacher told us to write about some people who live in another country. I got the encyclopedia and looked it up."

"Well, aren't the Arawak Indians in the encyclopedia?" Bob asked.

"Oh, sure, they're there all right."

"Aren't they poor and starving?" Mrs. Fulton asked. "I think it's wonderful the way they send clothes to those——"

"No, they're *not* poor and starving, Mother," Jennifer blubbered, "because they're *dead!*

121

They're all gone! The Spaniards killed all the Araw-w-whatevertheyare three hundred years ago!"

Bob jumped up from the table and ran from the room. In a few minutes he was back with Volume 12 of the Britannica. "She's right," he announced. "Page 873: 'In 1509 . . . blah . . . blah . . . Columbus stranded . . . blah . . .' Here it is: '. . . during the Spanish occupation the inoffensive Arawak inhabitants were exterminated and the tribe thereupon became extinct.' " He slammed the book shut.

"Come to think of it, I've never laid eye on an Arrywak in all my travels," the Captain observed.

"So you are not going to pick on poor Ingrid and Annie for that, are you?" Mrs. Fulton said. "There must be some explanation. After all, one doesn't mail lots of packages abroad just for the fun of it."

"No, Mom, you're right. My guess is they are mixed up in some fake charity racket. I've read about how people collect money from innocent donors and then keep most of it themselves. That's the only reason I can think of why they'd be mailing packages to nonexistent Indians."

"All right, Robert," she snapped back at her son. "That will be enough of that. I want no more

talk by you and your sister about our nice neighbors. Spies, liars, racketeers, indeed!"

"Well, all right, Mom. I've got enough to keep
me busy, anyway, without worrying about
them."

Thus Bob, as most of us would have done in the
same situation, failed to connect the strange behavior of the knitting ladies with the missing
Zeta or with any of his own activities.

13. The Start of Production

As time wore on, Bob had less and less opportunity to think about the Arawaks or any other Indians. He was spending hours every day in the laboratory, bringing the model Pop Stretcher to completion. Professor Narkus checked regularly on his progress.

"*Ach, himmel,* Robert!" he would say. "If this doesn't work . . ." He would slap his forehead, and Bob would become more nervous than ever.

The Professor also reported to Bob that the amount of Zeta residue taken from the rags had not been sufficient to conduct a thorough analysis of its make-up. But with what they knew, and with Bob's fairly useful list of ingredients, they had arrived at a formula to distill in the Giant Pop Stretcher when it was built—$C_{13}H_{23}O_{12}$—no telling what it would produce.

The moment finally arrived when the boy finished. The model Pop Stretcher rested on his workbench—a neat gadget that might have been a toy. It resembled the one that had blown up, but it was much smaller. As accurate as it was, it was not a working model. Its tiny pipes and petcocks were too narrow to carry any distilled liquid like Zeta. Its tank, bottle, and burner had hardly any capacity at all. Yet, as far as Bob could see from his careful work, this miniature machine was an exact duplicate of the original and would do perfectly for the SNURP experiments.

So Bob prepared to carry the model to Sandy Neck, where it would be used as a guide to the construction of a huge Pop Stretcher. He disconnected a few joints, and the Pop Stretcher came apart. He then opened a velvet-lined leather case and carefully placed the parts inside. He packed it with rags to prevent damage, closed the case, and snapped the lock. He then picked it up by the handle and walked to the town dock, where he boarded the ferry.

He was carrying his old tuba case. Bob once had practiced the tuba, trying to get into the school band, but never could blow hard enough

*The bottle part of the machine
reared into the sky ...*

to make any noise. In despair, he had convinced his mother to sell the tuba, but he had kept the case. At last he had found a use for it: it was good for carrying model Pop Stretchers!

At SNURP headquarters Professor Narkus greeted Bob with enthusiasm. "*Salaam,* Robert, how good to see you and how good to receive this."

He accepted the tuba case, opened it, and placed the parts on his desk. Bob carefully screwed the valves and joints back together and then explained to the Professor the method of operation. He also gave him a carefully written list of ingredients and directions.

"*Bravo,* Robert! The gang here at SNURP will get on the job at once. And when the Giant Pop Stretcher is built, you shall be here to help us get it going."

Bob returned home with the empty tuba case. He stowed it away in his laboratory. Only a few mornings after that he looked out of the kitchen window and saw some unfamiliar spires rising above the treetops on Sandy Neck. A few days later he recognized the structural steelwork as a gigantic edition of the Pop Stretcher tank. Soon after that, the immense sphere that represented the "bottle" part of the machine reared into the sky over the island.

A week later came the call. "This is it, Robert. Tomorrow we turn on the Pop Stretcher."

"I'll be there, Professor."

Bob rode the first ferry to Sandy Neck the following day. The Giant Pop Stretcher could be seen towering over the island. Captain Fulton told his son that it was visible all the way along the Cape from Provincetown to Sandwich. It was an impressive sight. At first Bob had an uneasy feeling that something was different, that something was missing, but he blamed this on his poor memory and forgot it.

At the landing Bob was met by Professor Narkus, who spoke to the Captain. "Come along, Captain. I want you to join in the ceremony too."

The three of them mushed through the stand to the gate and were admitted. The huge machine loomed over them. Where Bob had fashioned tiny pipes and faucets, there were tremendous valves and wheels. The huge tank and bottle were connected by sluices and ducts of large diameter. Beneath the tank was a blower-and-heating unit of some kind, and under the bottle was an empty reservoir, into which the Zeta-plus would flow, if all went well.

Bob and the others took their places at the control panel. He was explaining as much as he could to his father. He pointed off to the left, where a row of ten-ton trucks were lined up, engines idling.

"They'll dump that into the conveyer belt, Dad, and the belt will carry it to the top, where it will be deposited into the tank. Then, with pressure generated——"

"All right," shouted the Professor, "let her go!" He fiddled with several switches on the board in front of him. "And *Deus nobiscum*," he prayed under his breath.

The conveyer belt began to rumble. Beneath the tank flames shot out as the oil-fired heater ignited. The first real action to be seen was when a man deposited a wheelbarrow load of brown material into the belt. It was carried slowly upward in a crooked line.

"What could that be, lad?" asked the Captain.

"That's the original Zeta formula—we hope. A concoction of ginger, sassafras, and so forth."

Another worker then uncorked a gallon jug of thick brown liquid and poured it onto the belt; it stuck to the belt and slanted its way toward the top.

"That's Coca-Cola extract, Dad. You'll remember that I was stretching a Coke when she blew up. We are trying to re-create the exact conditions prevailing at that time."

Then with a roar the trucks began backing up

129

and dumping their contents onto the belt. One after another, until twelve of them had done so.

"What in blazes is all that?" the Captain demanded.

"Sugar. That's the principal component. We're starting with one hundred twenty tons of sugar. If that's not enough, we'll add more."

"By the Lord Harry!" Captain Fulton whistled. "That would sweeten a lot of tea!"

The Giant Pop Stretcher began belching smoke in a few minutes. The crew shouted "Hurrah!" and waved their hats in the air. The Professor and Bob were relieved to see the machine apparently working.

"Well, Bob, we've done it," the scientist congratulated his friend. "I think it'll be a few days before we can test the product. It'll have to cook at least that long, don't you agree?"

Bob nodded. "Yes. Projecting the data of my smaller machine to the large one—I make it that at least seventy-two hours will be needed to reach the proper point of congealment."

As Bob sailed back to the mainland, he stood on the stern of the *Clermont* and gazed back at the smoking Pop Stretcher. Once again he felt something was missing, that he had neglected to make a completely accurate model of his original device. He was still standing there, musing over

"That would sweeten a lot of tea!"

this vague uneasiness, when he heard his father's shouts.

"Avast! Land ho!"

At the same time there was a shattering crash and the *Clermont* bounced sideways, it seemed, as it hit the town landing piles. Bob's feet were thrown out from under him and he toppled over the side and into the water. He came up sputtering. In the customary confusion of the docking, no one noticed him. He dog-paddled a few feet to the ladder that led up to the town dock. As he pulled his soaking form to the dock itself, he attracted the attention of his father, who was just coming down the gangway.

"Why, son, this is no time for takin' a dip. And with y'r shoes on, too. Let's get ye home and into some dry duds." He chuckled.

"It's okay, Dad," Bob said with a wry smile. "I like to swim, you know."

They both walked toward the house, neither saying what was really in his mind.

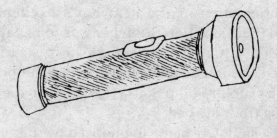

14. Danger for Bob Fulton

Bob heard nothing more from SNURP. Each morning he looked in the direction of Sandy Neck to see the smoke floating off to one side as the wind carried it into the sky. He knew that the machine was operating, distilling and building up pressure, and that soon the time would come to test it, to learn if it would produce the remarkable friction-eliminating Zeta-plus.

In the meantime, Bob amused himself by studying the knitting ladies across the street. Were they violating the statutes that govern donations to charity? After all, they had collected money and old clothes for a long time from the people of Barnstable, supposedly to forward them to the Arawaks. It wasn't fair to cheat.

The third night after the Pop Stretcher went into operation Bob stirred in bed, unable to sleep in anticipation of the next day's excitement, when the Giant Pop Stretcher was to be tapped for Zeta-plus—he hoped. As he tossed and turned, he found himself staring at the photograph of John Philip Sousa that hung on the wall across from his bed.

He was slowly being hypnotized by this, when his drowsy mind asked a question: "I've never been able to see Sousa with the lights out, how can I now?"

Bob then realized that a light from outside was coming through the window of his room. He climbed out of bed, looked out, and saw that the porch light of Ingrid and Annie's house was on. Inside, he could see some activity.

"Just what are those fake Arawak-helpers up to at this hour of the morning?" he wondered. "Now I'll never get to sleep, thinking about this."

Bob was thoroughly aroused. He looked at his alarm clock: 3 A.M. Soon it would be getting light. He pulled on his clothes and sneaked downstairs, through the kitchen and out the back way.

Coming out into the driveway, he had to feel

134

He found himself staring at the photograph of John Philip Sousa . . .

his way, for it was still rather dark. His plan was to reach the corner of the house, where he could look directly into the knitters' front windows to see what he could see. In the distance he could hear the belching and hissing of the Giant Pop Stretcher, as the sounds carried across the silent water.

Suddenly, passing the garage, he saw something out of the corner of an eye. He turned. It was a tiny spot of light from the laboratory-garage! Someone was inside! He reached for the padlock and found it hanging open, and the doors ajar.

His heart thumping, Bob carefully pushed his way inside. He couldn't see a thing except the vague outline of some person back in the corner inspecting the area with a pencil flashlight. As the boy stood there, hesitating about his next move, his arm pushed the old door one fraction of an inch too much and it squeaked! In the stillness of the night the noise was like the report of a rifle.

The flashlight was quickly focused directly on Bob's face.

"*Caramba!*" cried a voice. "What ees thees?" The light slowly came closer and closer as the person carrying it stepped toward Bob, who was transfixed by the glare and seemingly unable to move.

"Wh-who are you?" he asked.

"You shall soon see, my fran'," the voice said, and with that the speaker leaped at Bob. The boy, seeing what was coming, stepped lightly to one side, but the intruder's fist struck him on the side of the head. Bob went down and the man was on top of him, trying to kneel on his forearms and pin him down.

But the man, quick as he was, was no match for Bob. He kicked with one foot, arched his body in the middle, and threw the stranger heavily to one side. Then Bob scrambled over and fell on the fellow.

The two grunted and groaned as they punched and slapped at each other. It was a most unusual battle for Bob, at least, for it was being conducted in the dark. The flashlight lay over to one side, offering very little illumination for the struggle.

"Now, let's see what this is all about, mister," Bob said, after he had pinned the other down with a scissors grip. He pulled one of the man's arms behind his back and up, in a hammerlock; the intruder was completely helpless. "All right, get up," Bob ordered.

The man struggled to his knees as best he

The man struggled to his knees
as best he could . . .

could, considering the death grip Bob had on him. Bob dragged him over to where he could reach the electric switch. He snapped it, and the laboratory was flooded with light. For the first time he saw his antagonist, who was a man about thirty years old, thin but powerfully built, as Bob could now testify. He was dressed entirely in black, even to his sneakers, and his face was daubed with charcoal or some like substance which added to his spooky appearance. Bob had never seen him before.

"Who are you? What do you want?" Bob put pressure on the arm.

"Please, my fran', not so hard. I tell you." He spoke with an accent. "First, lat me go. I no harm you. I here to halp you."

"Burglarizing my lab and jumping me doesn't look like help. I think I'll just hang on here until I hear your story."

Before the black-garbed intruder could answer, Bob detected a strange whine in the distance. It was like no other noise he could identify. It seemed to increase in intensity, yet it was far away. Bob forced his prisoner over to where he could push open the garage doors further without losing his grip. He listened. The whine came from across the water; it was becoming a shriek.

The man in his grip looked up involuntarily, as

if an airplane were overhead. This tickled Bob's memory, and he knew he had heard the noise before. Like a jet plane! Like the first Pop Stretcher explosion in his garage! It was the Giant Pop Stretcher, shrieking from across the water. Something was wrong! And then Bob remembered what the defect was in the huge contraption. Oh, no!

Bob was so startled by the recollection that he relaxed his hold on the man in black, who suddenly executed a neat defensive maneuver, kicking backward with a heel, twisting up and over until he was free. At the same time he had jerked Bob's leg out from under him, and in those few seconds the tables had turned. Bob was flat on his own stomach, securely held down with a leg hold.

The fellow seized a length of line that happened to be within reach, looping it around Bob's ankles and neck in such a way that his struggles merely tightened the bonds more. Bob lay there panting, with one cheek in the dirt.

"You fool!" he cried. "Whoever you are, do you hear that noise? That's the Giant Pop Stretcher! When that goes, we're done for! I'm the only one who can fix it. Let me go!"

The man, who was running a comb through his dark hair, paused, surprised, but only for a moment. He quickly grabbed a dirty rag and stuffed it in Bob's mouth. He took another length of cloth and tied it around Bob's head to hold in the gag. Then he stood up, brushed himself, and re-arranged his mussed-up clothing, tucking his black shirt inside the waistband of his black trousers.

"You weesh to know who I am? I tell you, seence I leave now and you nevair see me again. I am Fidel Fundamento, ze numbair one spy of ze Caribbean. My apologies. I have no time for ze small talk. My orders: bring back ze model Stretchair from ze Fulton garage. As customary I, Fidel Fundamento, complete ze mission. And when ze Giant blows up, I am far away."

He grabbed the tuba case, picked up the flashlight, and raced out of the door.

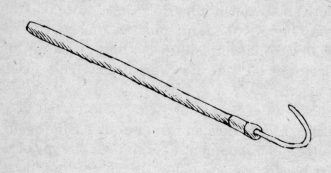

15. "Tit for Tat!"

The Fulton boy lay there, struggling with his bonds and trying to shout through the gag. It was no use. He had three reactions.

One was disgust at being beaten in the fight with the spy.

The second was slight amusement, for in his haste Fidel had made a mistake. The model was still over at Professor Narkus' office. The tuba case was empty.

Third, Bob was frightened, as the screaming continued.

Now he knew why the Giant machine had not looked absolutely right to him. He had forgotten to include a safety valve on the model! There was, therefore, no such device on the big Pop Stretcher. This meant it had been boiling, distilling, and building up pressure for three days and there was no way to relieve it. An explosion would devastate Sandy Neck, and probably kill or injure everyone within range. It could go off any time within the next few hours if something weren't done to reduce pressure.

How long he lay there with these horrible thoughts, he did not know. It was starting to get light outside. He heard a noise at the door and, looking up, saw his father standing there in his pajamas.

"What in——" his father began. He rushed over and released the boy. Bob jumped to his feet.

"No time to explain, Dad! Hurry! Get your things on and take me to Sandy Neck!"

As they hurried back to the house so he could dress, Captain Fulton told Bob that the telephone had awakened him. Professor Narkus was calling frantically for Bob to come to the Neck and help them with the runaway Pop Stretcher.

"I searched from stem to stern, finally seein' the lights in the garage. What in tarnation happened?"

"I'll tell you all about it on the way, Dad."

Shortly the two men were at the town dock. Bob cast off, while the Captain made for the

He rushed over and released the boy.

wheelhouse of the *Clermont*. Fortunately, there was steam up. Bob, who knew something about it, climbed down into the little engine room and checked the gauges. He went to the signal and called through the pipe to his father.

"There's enough to get going, Dad. I'll give you full speed ahead."

"Aye-aye, m'lad."

Bob pulled the big lever, and the two pistons began hissing and pushing up and down. The propeller shaft, visible in the bilge below, turned. Then Bob grabbed a shovel and began throwing coal into the firebox. He set the dampers. The fire glowed. The vessel rolled slightly as it moved. Soon the screw was turning her regular 78 rpm's.

When they were well under way, the boy climbed out and forward along the deck to the pilothouse. He stepped inside and stood next to the Captain at the wheel. There was a gray light coming from the east, but the water was still dark. The *Clermont*'s lights sparkled. In the distance they could see—and hear—the Pop Stretcher against the sky.

"Now, what's the story?" the Captain asked.

Bob described the incident to his father, who whistled in disbelief when he heard about the spy, Fidel Fundamento. Bob then revealed the sad news about the missing safety valve on the big machine at Sandy Neck.

"Great jumpin' Jehoshaphat!" the Captain cried.

"And to think, I was wasting my time worrying about Ingrid and Annie and their silly Arawak Indians when there was *real* danger lurking in the area!" Bob said.

"We told you, son: those old ladies are harmless as a furled spanker in the doldrums."

The vessel knifed through the water. In his haste to reach the Neck by the shortest route, Captain Fulton forgot about the channel and simply headed straight for the island. Buoys and flashing markers meant nothing to him; moored boats rocked in the wash as he cut close to them. Luckily the tide was high, or they'd have hit Goose Rock. But at one point the sharp prow of the *Clermont* seemed to be bearing directly down on some dark object ahead.

"Watch out, Dad, you're not going to miss this one."

As they came closer, they could see better what it was. A little craft of some sort bobbed on the water. In it a figure was in violent motion. They were almost upon it when Bob, who had run out on deck, recognized a person all in black. It was Fidel, the spy! He was in a tiny rubber boat and he was rowing like mad to escape the onrushing steamboat. He tried to pull laterally out of the *Clermont*'s path.

The Captain stuck his head out of the wheel-house window. "Tell them two lubbers to get out of our way!"

"That's not two lubbers, Dad! That's Fidel the spy and the tuba case! Quick, run alongside!"

"Hard aport," the Captain cried, and swung the steamboat to the right, which happens to be star-board. Bob picked up a ten-foot boat hook. As the rubber dinghy came next to him, without any hesitation he tapped Fidel Fundamento on the head and the great spy collapsed in a heap. The oars fell overboard and floated away. In a quick move, Bob hooked onto the painter of the little craft and pulled it toward him. The *Clermont* raced along; the bow wave lifted the rubber boat up and down perilously.

Finally Bob managed to reach down and grab the rope. He carried it to the stern, where he cleated it. He called to his father, who swung the *Clermont* back onto its course to the island. Bob watched the unconscious spy being tossed this way and that, the rubber boat swinging from side to side in the wash. He grinned.

"Tit for tat, Mister Number One Spy."

In about ten or fifteen minutes they were close

"That's Fidel the spy and the tuba case!"

enough to the Sandy Neck docking area so that Bob had to get back into the engine room. He saw that Fidel hadn't moved and was still dead to the world, so he clambered down the steel ladder to await his father's orders. Finally came two bells. Bob looked at the sign on the bulkhead: "Two bells—half astern." He pushed the lever back. Then came a long jingle: "Full astern." Bob braced himself for the crash, as the ship shivered and shook under the strain of having the forty-inch, four-bladed propeller pulling against her forward motion.

But there was no crash, only a slight bump. Then came three long jingles over the telegraph: "Through with engines." Bob climbed out and saw to his amazement that his father had made a perfect landing. The *Clermont* was settled snugly against the dock. Professor Narkus and some others were hurriedly making fast the ship's lines.

"Kuai-kuai te!" the scientist shouted in Chinese to Bob. "Hurry!" He could hardly be heard above the whine of the Pop Stretcher.

Bob jumped to the dock. "Just a minute, Professor. Look!" He pulled the scientist down to the stern, where he pointed to the unconscious heap in the rubber boat. Quickly he told the Professor all that had happened.

"Pukka sahib!" he congratulated Bob in Hindustani. "But there's no time for this. We must relieve the pressure on the Stretcher or we'll be blown to smithereens!" He spoke to one of the men with him. "Edgar, phone up to the internal security office. Tell them there's a captured foreign agent here." He pointed to Fidel.

Edgar nodded and rushed to the nearby phone booth. The Professor grabbed Bob's arm and pushed him along toward the SNURP area inland. The noise became more intense. When they finally reached the platform and the control panel, the Giant Pop Stretcher was almost totally obscured by the escaping steam. It shot from the fittings where the pipes were joined, and to his dismay Bob could see that even the riveted plates of the main tank were beginning to seep.

Obviously, the dangerous mechanism was ready to give way!

16. Two Unexpected Stowaways

"What do you make of that?" the Professor yelled in Bob's ear.

"The trouble with that machine is there's no safety valve!" the boy yelled back. The steam swirled around them.

"No safety valve! *Kiswaste?*"

Bob confessed that he had forgotten about it when he made his model.

Professor Narkus began to grow red in the face, the way he did when his grouchiness got the better of him. But the racket from the Pop Stretcher spoiled the opportunity for a temper tantrum, so he merely shouted, "All right, what

"I'm going in!"

are you going to do about it? I've given up trying
to think of something."

"Did you cut out the burner?"

The Professor nodded.

"Stopped feeding her water?"

He nodded again.

"All right, give me that wrench!" Bob said.
"I'm going in." He jumped from the platform and
ran through the vapor until he was directly under
the huge machinery of the Giant Pop Stretcher.
He knew that if he could loosen the double-
jointed feed pipe that led from the tank to the
reservoir, it would release a lot of pressure and
probably save the day. He hoped he wouldn't get
scalded in the process.

He was fitting the wrench to the lock nut on the
joint, when he smelled something familiar. What
was that? He groped in the direction from which
the smell came, beneath the reservoir, and saw
that the outflow tap was leaking slightly. From it
dripped a gummy goo that looked like, smelled
like, and—as Bob rubbed it between his fingers
—felt like *Zeta-plus!*

With a happy cry, he dropped the wrench and
ran back to the platform. "Professor," he cried,
"that contraption is ready to be tapped! Get your
men down there to the main outlet!"

As it turned out, Bob was exactly right. The

Pop Stretcher was acting up because it was like a cow that needed milking—it was loaded with Zeta-plus. Not long after the men had tapped the reservoir, the pressure was off, and slowly a small container filled with the gooey liquid. The silence was eerie, after that endless screeching.

Bob and the Professor walked back to the dock. The sun had risen and the Cape lay before them, a white-and-green strand with the blue water stretching along in front.

The man put an arm on his friend's shoulders. "Well, Bob, we shall soon know whether we can present the nation with another great scientific advance—frictionless bearings. And, I might say, it is in no small measure due to your efforts. Of course, the implications of this invention in the space race and in the military picture are immense. It's no wonder that spies from foreign powers are already exercising their wiles to obtain the secret."

Bob thanked the Professor for his praise. They reached the landing, where Captain Fulton stood holding the empty tuba case. He reported that the spy, Fidel, had been locked up in the SNURP guardhouse and that he would be questioned later. The rubber boat had been confiscated and would be held as evidence. The *Clermont* would take it back to Barnstable for safekeeping.

"All right, son, let's get under way," the Captain ordered. In a few minutes the *Clermont* plowed back toward the mainland, with Bob manning the engine room as before. He looked at his watch. Six. His alarm would be going off just about now. Think of all that had happened already that day!

At the town dock Captain Fulton stayed aboard to make ready for the first scheduled crossing of the day. His son yawned and walked up the lane toward his own house. He carried the tuba case with him. He glanced in the direction of the house across the street. To his surprise, the knitting ladies were at work already, at that early hour. They nodded and Bob waved.

Although Ingrid and Annie rocked and knitted, they were in earnest conversation, whispering hoarsely to each other between their teeth.

"Did you see that?" Ingrid said.

"He's got the model with him! What could have gone wrong? Fidel left at 3 A.M. He should be out to sea by now."

"Listen, Annie. Get up slowly and walk casually into the house. Get into your boots. We're going clamming."

"Clamming? What ever for?"

"I want to retrace Fidel's movements. Now do as I say," Ingrid muttered severely.

Annie stopped rocking, folded her knitting, and shuffled inside. Ingrid stretched and said loudly, "Well, let's go dig clams." She followed her friend indoors. Hastily they climbed into their boots, grabbed their clam rakes and pails, and made for Phinney's Lane. They kept their knitting bags with them, too, for they never let them out of their sight.

The women were a strange picture, shuffling down to the town dock area with that paraphernalia, and in their peculiar garb. Ingrid led the way, going right down to the water's edge among the rocks and mud. She waded into the water until the water came almost to her boot tops. Then she began raking. Annie followed suit. It was so early they were completely alone. Ingrid's eyes were anyplace but on the muddy gunk she brought up from the bottom. Rather, she was searching the waterfront for something.

As her eyes roved back and forth, they fell upon the rubber craft resting on the fantail of the *Clermont*. She gave a cry and her hand went to her throat.

"Annie, Annie!" she whispered, pointing. "Look! Fidel's rubber boat! They've captured him. Oh, poor Fidel! Oh, oh, what can we do?"

Annie's face turned pale. "The heck with Fidel," she growled. "We'd better clear out, that's

The women were a strange picture ...

what." She dropped her rake and pail and waded frantically toward shore. The water went over her boots and inside, sloshing around.

"Come back here, you idiot!" Ingrid ordered, recovering her composure.

Annie, accustomed to taking orders from Ingrid, halted and did what she was told. Ingrid looked around; there wasn't a soul in sight. She led Annie toward the ferryboat.

"We'll finish this rendezvous ourselves, even if it is without Fidel. It's too late to get the model Pop Stretcher, but we must pass along the word about what happened. We'll rendezvous with that submarine ourselves—just you and I."

"And make a getaway, too," Annie insisted.

"Come on, help me get this into the water." They climbed aboard the *Clermont* and began wrestling with Fidel's rubber boat.

"Wait a minute," Annie said. "There are no oars."

"Well, let's find them." The women poked around the deck for a minute until Ingrid froze. "Someone's coming! Quick, in here!" They pushed their way into a hatchway and found themselves in a tiny cabin just behind the pilot-house. They crouched down, huddling near each other, trying to breathe quietly. There was a stomping on the deck above them.

"F-ul-ton," Ingrid formed the word with her lips. Annie nodded. Then they heard voices. Mr. Bones had come aboard. Soon there were the sounds of passengers and the cries of the Captain as he got his ship under way for the passage to Sandy Neck. They could hear him banging around in the wheelhouse, separated from the tiny cabin only by a heavy burlap curtain. They realized now that they were hiding in the Captain's quarters.

"What do we do now?" Annie whispered directly into Ingrid's eardrum.

Ingrid gave her friend a determined look, opened her knitting bag, and reached way down to the bottom. When her hand came out, it held a mean-looking automatic pistol. Ingrid grasped it like a veteran. With her thumb she snapped off the safety catch. She got to her feet and started up the few steps to the pilothouse, pointing the muzzle directly at the burlap curtain that separated her from Captain Fulton.

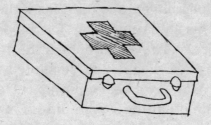

17.   Adventure on the High Seas

"Fifteen men on a dead man's chest!
Yo-ho-ho and a bottle of rum!"

Captain Fulton was singing one of his favorite
sea chanteys as he guided the *Clermont* through
Barnstable Harbor, blasting the whistle and scat-
tering the smaller craft that wisely got out of the
way when they saw her coming.

The Captain fished a worn piece of paper out of
a cubbyhole and studied it. "Port-left; starboard-
right," he read. He repeated this to himself a few
times after he had tucked the slip back into its
regular hiding place. Just then he felt a move-

ment of air directly behind him. He glanced back and saw that he was not alone.

"Well, flog me around the fleet!" he cried. "We have company. Good morning, ladies, what a pleasant surprise. It's a little early in the day for that moonlight cruise, but welcome aboard." The Captain wrestled with the wheel and kept his attention on the *Clermont*'s course. "Now, just where would you be wantin' to go?"

"We want to cruise out into Cape Cod Bay," Ingrid declared grimly.

"Ye don't say! Now wouldn't that be somethin'! All these here passengers booked for Sandy Neck, and old Cap Fulton takes 'em to Cape Cod Bay. Ho, ho, ho! I guess ye'll have to cancel your plans, m'ladies."

He felt something cold pressed against the back of his neck.

"All right, my one-eyed friend," Ingrid's voice was menacing. "This firearm is loaded. You will follow my instructions. Proceed past the island and into the open water. No funny business."

The man slowly turned around and for the first time saw the serious expressions on the faces of the two knitters. He looked directly into the barrel of the gun.

"Now, looky here! What kind of hogwash is

"Good morning, ladies!"

this? Why don't you two just get back to saving the poor starving Arrywaks—if there truly be any such critters?"

Ingrid jammed the gun into his ribs. "Do as you're told, you ridiculous man, or be a dead hero!"

"Blast ye! This is piracy on the high seas! Ye'll hang from the Queen's scaffold for this!" He went back to the wheel.

"How many passengers are there?" Annie asked.

"Four," he replied sullenly.

"And the crew?"

"A deckhand and a fireman."

"Annie, switch on the loudspeakers," Ingrid ordered, without easing the pressure of the gun barrel in the Captain's side. Annie reached for the controls and flipped a switch. She held the microphone to his lips.

"Explain to them there is nothing wrong," Ingrid whispered. "Just a slight detour while we deliver a special cargo out in the Bay."

The Captain hesitated. She stuck the gun hard into him and he jumped. He licked his lips and cleared his throat.

"Now hear this!" he announced. "This is your skipper speaking. We shall follow a different course on this trip. We'll make Sandy Neck after a stop in Cape Cod Bay. That is all."

"Good," Ingrid said. "Now, Annie, onto the wireless and get in touch with the S-50. You know the frequency."

Annie nodded, flipped switches and spun dials on the radio, and soon was in rapid-fire conversation in a foreign language which Captain Fulton recognized as Spanish. He couldn't understand what was said.

As Annie turned off the transmitter, the ladies carefully directed the Captain out through the narrow channel, past a bell buoy marked No. 2, straight out into the expanse of the Bay. They steamed until they were a few miles from land. Then Ingrid ordered, "Stop engines!" The Captain did as he was told, and the *Clermont* drifted idly for several minutes while the trio remained tensely in the wheelhouse. The passengers on the rear deck showed no interest in the situation at all.

Suddenly there was an unusual disturbance in the water about a hundred yards off the beam. A huge gray form burst out of the blue water. Captain Fulton's eye popped.

"A submarine!"

"Right, my friend," Annie said. She waved out the window to the men who scrambled out of the sub's conning tower and onto her deck. They put over a small boat, and a man rowed quickly to the *Clermont*. Everyone on the ferry hung in amazement over the rail as the two ladies backed toward the side and climbed into the boat.

Just as Ingrid stepped down, the Captain noted that the gun was pointed away from the steamer. Bravely he rushed at her. But she was too quick for him. She jerked the muzzle of her weapon around and pulled the trigger. There was a shot, and the Captain fell heavily to the deck.

"Let that be a lesson to you!" she cried, as she and Annie were rowed back to the submarine. Captain Fulton lay there, groaning and holding his leg. Two passengers helped him to his feet and assisted him into the pilothouse.

"It's only a flesh wound," he said. They made a hasty bandage from the materials in the first-aid kit and stopped the flow of blood.

In the meantime, the little boat had been hauled onto the submarine and stowed away. The knitters had disappeared below. Then, to the astonishment of the persons on the ferry, the sub's crew manned the five-inch gun on her deck. They loaded it and aimed it directly at the *Clermont*.

"Man the lifeboats!" Captain Fulton shouted when he saw this. "Prepare to abandon ship!"

There was a mad rush as Mr. Bones and the one deckhand unlashed the dinghy and got ready to lower it over the side. A voice from across the water stopped them. The sub's commander was calling to them through a megaphone.

"Hold it!" he ordered. "We shall not fire upon you, if you co-operate. You will be so kind, Captain, as to give us a course out of this bay and into the ocean. My charts are not very good. But let me warn you. If you trick me, I shall return and blow you out of the water."

"Well, of all the dad-blasted nerve!" Captain Fulton growled. "If that free-bootin' blackguard thinks that old Cap Fulton——"

"For crying out loud, tell him, Captain!" yelled one of the passengers. The others shouted similar suggestions.

The Captain hesitated, then flipped on the public address system. He held the mike in one hand and poked his finger at the chart. "Directly north to Black Can No. 45. Then north-northeast. That'll take you into the ocean. Be sure and pass to the right of Obstruction Buoy No. 12!"

"Thank you, Captain. You're a true man of the sea," replied the sub commander. He and the crew climbed into their ship, and in a few minutes it had dropped below the surface of the wa-

"You're a true man of the sea!"

ter, leaving a few bubbles to remind the group on the *Clermont* of their fantastic adventure.

Captain Fulton sat on a stool, trying to fathom why the two nice old ladies had sailed away in a submarine. His leg hurt and he wondered why someone who was so kind to Arrywak Indians would shoot him. As he was thinking about this, Mr. Bones spoke.

"Say, Skipper, why did you tell him to keep RIGHT of No. 12?"

"Why not? I don't want to be shot. Do you?"

"No, but the clear channel is to the LEFT of that marker. Look here on the chart." His big grimy finger pointed.

"What?" the Captain cried. "Well, get below! Full speed ahead! Let's get out of here! Which way is land?" He swung the wheel.

18. World-shaking Developments

The *Clermont* steamed on to Sandy Neck without seeing any more of the submarine. Captain Fulton was taken to the base hospital, where his leg was treated. Professor Narkus, who had heard the news, came to visit.

"Well," he remarked with sympathy, "you Fultons have had your share of excitement today, haven't you? Espionage before breakfast and piracy after." He looked at the leg. *"Dard hota hai?"*

"Nov schmoz ka pop," the Captain replied without batting an eye. The Professor grunted and nodded, not wishing to admit that there was a language he did not understand.

"Have you any idea what this is all about?" he asked, referring to the hijacking incident.

"Negative. All I can figure is it's got somethin' to do with a fake charity racket the two women are mixed up in." He told the Professor all about the Arawak Indians.

"Probably they had to get out of the country before they were caught," the Professor mused. "Well, we've got our own problems here with that spy, Fidel. He refuses to talk and he's being sent to Washington for further questioning and investigation."

Fortunately, the gunshot wound was not serious. The Captain was able to continue immediately as master of the *Clermont,* and the ferry went back on its regular route without much disruption in schedule. The main disadvantage for him was that the bullet had hit him in his "good" leg. He was forced to limp on it. Since it is hard to limp on two legs at once, he had to give up his habit of stomping about on the "bad" leg, until the wound healed or stopped hurting.

However, for some strange reason nobody seemed to notice that after umpteen years of leaning to one side, the old salt was now tilting to the other as he walked. The Captain helped to cover up his embarrassment by switching the black patch to the other eye. This got people

"He's being sent to Washington
for further questioning."

thoroughly confused and no one said a word. The Captain was happy to discover that he could see much better.

There was a brief investigation into the affair by the Constable of Barnstable, after Captain Fulton had reported the incident to him. However, there was so little evidence to go on, that the local official was stumped. A search of the empty house proved that the knitters had left nothing of importance. (In his zeal, the Constable tasted some jam in a pail that made him sick.)

Another drawback, according to the officer, was that if any crime had been committed by the two women, it had occurred beyond the three-mile limit where the Constable's powers left off. Of course, the Constable knew nothing about Fidel, the spy, for that was a case for the SNURP security police. They, in turn, were not the least bit interested in two lady racketeers with knitting bags. No one saw any connection.

Captain Fulton felt, nevertheless, that there was so much lawlessness and disorder that he ought to be prepared. He armed himself with a shotgun, which he kept loaded and close at hand in the wheelhouse of the *Clermont*.

While all this was going on, the Giant Pop Stretcher gurgled and burbled on Sandy Neck. Thanks to Zeta-plus, the antigravity experiments went very well. Professor Narkus reported to Bob that lubricating the floating balls with Zeta-plus cut down much of the resistance. The vacuum tubes were then able to keep the balls suspended in their flight for a fraction of an instant longer than before. Even this was a tremendous step forward. From home, Bob could also see that the windmill—still operating without benefit of the wind—rotated much more effectively than before. It, too, had been given Zeta-plus.

The magic material had other uses. All government vehicles were greased with it. Jet engines, helicopters, warships, elevators, and hundreds of different kinds of machinery were treated to cut down friction resistance. The savings were enormous, in both time and fuel.

Bob lubricated the bearings and joints of the *Clermont*'s power plant with Zeta-plus. Designed and built a half century earlier by the Fore River Company of Weymouth, Massachusetts, the ancient engine took on new life. Mr. Bones couldn't open her up fully any more or the spinning propeller would shake the vessel to pieces. He also found that he could get along with about 30 pounds of pressure, rather than the usual 125. As a result, the use of fuel was cut to a minimum.

Professor Narkus told Bob about some other

things that happened. For instance, scientists had put Zeta-plus to a test on locomotive and passenger-car bearings. As a result, a New Haven Railroad express train had coasted from Providence, Rhode Island, to Grand Central Station—185.5 miles.

Another more startling indication of what might come about was revealed in a highly confidential memorandum from Detroit, Michigan. It was a stenographic report of a secret conference attended by the top executives in the automobile manufacturing business. Professor Narkus let Bob, the discoverer of Zeta-plus, see the report to show him how far-reaching his discovery could be. Here is what Bob read:

(*Transcript of Meeting.*)

AUTO MANUFACTURER: Gentlemen, I called you here to discuss this new friction-free bearing matter we've heard about from the Pentagon. Do you know what this means?

SECOND AUTO MANUFACTURER: I certainly do, J.B. It means we'll go out of business, that's what. Cars won't wear out; they'll use hardly any gasoline and no oil. There'll be no rattling, no sticky valves, and no loose pistons—why, folks will keep their cars for ten years or more. No trade-ins!

THIRD AUTO MANUFACTURER: We'll have to

make all our profits on brake linings and tires. That's no good.

FOURTH AUTO MANUFACTURER: Oh, we're done for, done for!

FIRST A.M.: Now, gentlemen, calm down. There is a way out of this hole, if you'll all go along.

THE OTHERS: There is? What? How? We'll go along, J.B.!

FIRST A.M.: Redesign our product.

SECOND A.M.: Redesign the cars?

THIRD A.M.: But that's what we've been doing, year after year.

FOURTH A.M.: Redesign our—oh, now we're really done for, done for!

FIRST A.M.: Stop your bawling and listen to me. This Zeta stuff may eliminate friction, but it can't do anything about wind resistance, can it? We've just got to *unstreamline* our vehicles, that's all. Build up the wind resistance again.

SECOND A.M.: You mean, with the big high windshields, the huge headlights, the fenders, the running boards a couple of feet off the ground, and all that? Well, I'll be darned!

THIRD A.M.: J.B., you're a genius! What are we waiting for? Let's go! Let's get to work! Get those old 1919 blueprints out of the files!

FOURTH A.M.: Oh, we're done for, done for!

(*End of Meeting.*)

There was no doubt about it: Zeta-plus had

"We've got to un-streamline our vehicles."

already had a profound effect on the lives of many Americans. Not only Detroit and Washington were revising plans, but even in the side roads of Barnstable life had changed. Kids with bicycles were speeding all over the place, passing cars on hills, racing along the Mid-Cape Highway, pumping on week ends to such places as Taunton, Massachusetts. This resulted from the fact that Bob Fulton still had a few Zeta-soaked rags in his garage which he used now and then to lubricate the bikes of Jennifer's friends.

His was probably the only civilian use of the formula in the country. Although the Sandy Neck machine turned out a big supply, most of it was reserved for the government projects. In the future, however, there was no doubt that Zeta-plus would be manufactured commercially. It would make the Fulton family independently wealthy.

And then one day—blooey!

The bubble burst and disintegrated almost as rapidly as it had appeared. The heroes of Sandy Neck, and this included Bob Fulton too, became villains. It was an amazing development in a summer that had certainly seen some amazing developments.

19. The General Signs a Treaty

A Barnstable boy called Tubby Nibset was the first to become aware of the situation. One hot day he entered his favorite hangout, the 6-A Confectionery Store & Ice Cream Shoppe, Inc., and ordered his usual—a triple malted chocolate special, known there as a Ball of Heavenly Delight.

The clerk looked at him and said, "Sorry, Tub, we're not servin' the Ball of Heavenly Delight any more."

Tubby's large frame shivered in disappointment and disbelief. "Not serving?"

"We're fresh out of sirup, ice cream, and maraschino cherries. Fact is, they tell us we can't expect any for quite a while."

Tubby Nibset didn't believe a word of this, because as long as he could remember there had always been ice cream, sirup, and maraschino cherries. He leaped upon his bicycle and raced home, where he confronted his mother.

"Whassa big idea, Mom? You told them at the 6-A not to let me eat any more stuff there? I'm hungry." He began to feel terribly sorry for himself.

"Why, Wilfred," his mother soothed, "I never told them anything of the sort. You poor boy. Here, have some lamb chops to keep you going until dinner. I'm sorry I don't have any of your favorite cake or pie, but I've been unable to get more than a pound of sugar at a time at the store."

A day or two after Tubby was thus saved from starvation, a crisis occurred elsewhere. General Horatio Gates stopped at the Sandy Neck Sandwich Nook to purchase his daily candy bar. He couldn't find it on the rack, so he asked for it.

"I'm afraid we haven't any, sir," said the girl behind the counter. "They haven't delivered any candy bars for about four days, and our supply is gone. What's more, I hear from Hershey, Pennsylvania, that the factory has closed down. The truck driver told me they can't get the supplies."

"Can't get the supplies?" echoed the General.

"What do they mean by that? Well, I'll have some gum, then."

"No gum, either, General. The Beech-Nut people have canceled all orders."

"What? Why this is ridiculous! These things are nothing more than flavoring and flour and sugar and—*sugar!*" The General's jaw dropped in shock. He turned and ran across the dunes toward the SNURP headquarters.

A moment later he was in conference with Professor Narkus. "Narkus," he asked, "just what is the exact ratio between the raw materials that go into the Pop Stretcher and the Zeta-plus that comes out?"

"Well, General, it takes about one hundred tons of $C_{22}H_{12}O_{11}$ to make an ounce of Zeta, in addition to smaller quantities of cola extract and——"

"Tell me, Professor, just what is the common name for $C_{22}H_{12}O_{11}$?"

"Why, I suppose most people call it cane sugar. *Pourquoi?*"

"One hundred tons!" The General whistled. "Come on, we've got to get in touch with the Pentagon, the White House, somebody. There's something we forgot."

But Tubby Nibset hadn't forgotten. After having gone practically five days without a Ball of Heavenly Delight, he was in a revolutionary mood. He had lost about ten pounds, not only from lack of nourishment, but from the exercise he got racing all over the Cape on his bicycle looking for a confectionery store or an ice cream fountain where they would sell him a malted, a sundae, a banana split—*anything*. He was unsuccessful.

On the last few of these foraging trips, looking for sweets, he was accompanied by the gang—a group of boys and girls from Barnstable whose systems ached for ice cream too. Even Jennifer Fulton was among them, mainly because it was her own brother who had made it possible for the gang to ride their bikes to faraway places.

One afternoon the gang was returning home, empty-handed, and they paused for a rest at the top of Shootflying Hill. As they looked down into the outskirts of town, they saw a strange sight. A big parking area was filled with trucks. All the trucks looked alike: painted white, with a little open cockpit for the driver, and a string of bells across the opening. Good Humor trucks!

"Look," said Tubby, pointing, "they are gathering rust. Even the Good Humor people can't get ice cream."

"My mother says it's because there isn't any sugar," said Jennifer. "She says they have started Russianing at the store."

"Communists are behind this candy shortage, you mean?" queried Tubby, a smart fellow.

"I guess so. Whatever it is, only one bag to a customer."

Tubby's eyes widened. As he gazed into the distance, he could see Barnstable Harbor filled with ships, most of them big freighters waiting to be unloaded at the SNURP docking facilities. Jennifer looked in the same direction.

"It's kinda silly, too," she finally said, "because those ships are just *filled* with sugar, my brother told me."

"That's what I was wondering," Tubby said. He turned to the gang of kids milling around and began to speak to them. In a few minutes the whole bunch was speeding toward Barnstable, with determined looks upon their faces.

The next morning Phinney's Lane was treated to an astonishing spectacle. As people arrived to catch the ferry to Sandy Neck, they found a parade of youngsters marching back and forth on the dock carrying placards and signs and shouting slogans.

"MORE GUM, CHUMS" read the sign held by Tubby Nibset.

*Phinney's Lane was treated to an
astonishing spectacle.*

"SNURP SWIPES SUGAR" declared another.

"GRAVITY, NO. CANDY, YES!" was a third.

Jennifer, Tubby, and the others circled the area, singing, "I scream, you scream, we all scream for ice cream!"

When Bob Fulton came along to start the day's work on board the *Clermont,* the howl intensified.

"There's the guy who started it all!" shouted Tubby.

The boy inventor was soon surrounded by the others, and he saw even his own sister shouting at him.

"What's it all about?" he yelled, slightly bewildered. The shouts quieted down, and Tubby told Bob how the sugar shortage had affected their lives.

"And we demand action!" Tubby concluded.

Just then Captain Fulton appeared. He was taken aback at the scene, but quickly sized up the situation.

"A picket line!" he cried. Bob told his father what the complaint was.

"Is that true, me lad?"

"Afraid so, Dad. The Pop Stretcher uses up sugar at a tremendous rate. It's quite possible that most of the nation's supply is going just for this one purpose."

"Well, I'll be—that makes about as much sense as a hull full of barnacles. Is Zeta-plus that important?"

Bob shrugged. "Sure, it's important. But they're trying to make as much as they can, so they can use it all over the place. If they'd just stick to the SNURP antigravity experiments, they wouldn't need much at all."

At that moment there was a screech of brakes as a military car swept up to the crowd, which by now was quite large. General Gates hopped out and strode toward the landing.

"All right," he ordered in his most officious manner, "dismiss this platoon. Let's go, Captain, to Sandy Neck and hurry!"

Captain Fulton tugged at his beard and said, "Not sailing today, General. Old Cap Fulton never crosses a picket line."

"Picket line? Picket line? What are you talking about?" Then for the first time General Gates inspected the signs and the little people who were carrying them. "Why this is an outrage! I'll have you court-martialed for this insubordination. I'll——"

"We're not in the Army, General," the Captain replied.

Then there was a rattling and popping up the lane. It was Professor Narkus approaching in his old rattletrap. He parked and came over to the scene of action. He greeted his friends, but was startled when the boys and girls surrounded him with their placards and chanted, "We want sugar! We want sugar!"

General Gates grabbed the Professor by the arm and pulled him away from the gang. He jerked his head at Bob, indicating that he should join them. They hurried into the Fulton driveway and into the garage. In a few seconds the General had explained the impasse.

"And I've just come back from the White House," he said intensely. "I've got to get over to the Pop Stretcher to cut down on her capacity. It seems that the country is in a turmoil over this sugar shortage. And we didn't realize it. The Pentagon is up in arms. They haven't had any desserts at officers' mess for two weeks. Do you realize that this machine has been eating up ninety per cent of the sugar output of the United States? But with those little devils out there, how can we get to SNURP headquarters?"

"Why not just tell them the shortage will come to an end?" Bob suggested.

"Yes, I suppose that's all I need do. Professor, if we scale our production just to satisfy the antigravity experiments, how would that affect our use of raw cane sugar?"

"Hmmm," Professor Narkus figured in his head. "We're now using about eighteen hundred tons a day. I think we could get along on much less, in that case."

"Great!" cried the General. "That's what I told them in Washington. All right, let's break up this little roadblock."

The three men walked out to the howling mob, where the General quieted them down.

"I have assurances from Washington," he announced, "that you will soon find sugar and its by-products back on your shelves. The Pop Stretcher will be slowed down. Now, let's get on with the show." He started for the *Clermont*. But he didn't get very far.

Tubby Nibset shouted, "Oh, no! None of those promises! How do we know you're tellin' the truth?"

"Yeah, how do we know?" cried the others.

"Put it in writing!" shouted someone.

That is how the most amazing thing happened. In the quiet of the laboratory-garage where Bob Fulton had begun the whole crazy business a few weeks before, General Gates sat down at a makeshift desk, facing Wilfred "Tubby" Nibset, the representative of a candy-hungry rabble. They drafted and signed a treaty, in which General Gates, speaking for the United States Government, agreed to reduce drastically the manufacture of Zeta-plus.

Tubby Nibset ran out to the gang, waving his copy of the treaty, shouting, "Sweets for the sweet!"

Everybody cheered. Captain Fulton and Bob got steam up on the ferry, and by the end of the day the Giant Pop Stretcher was gurgling and fizzing just a little bit, enough to make Zeta-plus for SNURP and nothing more.

20. Lost in a Fog

The Labor Day week end was a pretty exciting one for certain people in Barnstable. On that Monday a local boy, Robert Farragut Fulton, was to be presented with a Certificate of Merit by officials of the Sandy Neck Uphill Rectification Project. The certificate was in honor of a certain contribution the young man had made to the space effort. Everyone knew that remarkable discoveries concerning gravity had come from the Zeta-plus formula invented by the young Fulton boy. The ceremony, therefore, would probably be attended by all sorts of well-wishers.

The weather wasn't too good. Mrs. Fulton, Bob, and Jennifer were dressed in their best clothes, but they carried raincoats in case the skies opened up, which surely seemed likely. They had to catch the early ferry so they could be at Sandy Neck in time for the presentation. As they boarded the *Clermont*, they saw many friends and neighbors who were also going to the affair.

The Fultons found seats in the cabin, since it was too foggy and damp to stand on deck. But the boat was so crowded that many passengers were forced to remain outside. There was an overflow into such places as the tiny forecastle and Captain Fulton's quarters. Professor Narkus and other SNURP officials lined the rails up forward.

As lines were being singled up and the *Clermont* was starting to move, there was a commotion on the dock. A flashing red light could be seen through the mist—an official car of some kind. Three figures appeared. One of them called to the Captain to hold his departure. The ferry was maneuvered closer to the dock, a gangway was lowered, and the three figures pushed on board. Observers were astonished to note that one was a strangely dressed fellow—in black from head to toe—in handcuffs.

Wondering about the delay, Bob peeked out of the cabin porthole and saw the late arrivals.

"Well, I'll be darned," he muttered. "Fidel Fundamento! I'll be right back."

He left the cabin and went on deck. The gangplank had been removed again, and the boat was moving out into the dense fog. Bob found Professor Narkus, who explained that apparently the authorities in Washington were sending the spy back to Sandy Neck for further questioning. They watched the two escorts hustle Fidel into the Captain's quarters, after having cleared out the passengers who had taken it over. Bob saw that the fellow was dressed exactly as he had been on the night of their battle. He chatted a few minutes with Professor Narkus, who revealed that the security police had been unable to connect Fidel with any spy ring. They couldn't even find out which Caribbean country he worked for. He might have to be released for lack of evidence.

"Released!" Bob exclaimed. "He stole the Pop Stretcher model. That's espionage, isn't it?"

"*Eheu!* He stole a tuba case. So far all he can be charged with is burglary and assault and battery. That isn't a federal crime, son."

Bob returned to his seat in the cabin with a disappointed look on his face.

"What's wrong, sonny?" his mother inquired.

Bob quickly told her the situation. "So it appears that Fidel Fundamento, the number one spy of the Caribbean, will go scot free."

Jennifer looked up from her coloring book. "Fidel who?"

"All he can be charged with is burglary and assault and battery."

Bob waved his hand in a disgusted way at his little sister. "Nobody you know."

She went back to her coloring. "Oh, I thought you said Fundamento."

"Maybe we could get him for burglary," Bob explained to his mother, "and for——" He turned to his sister. "I did say Fundamento. Why?"

"Oh, nothing." She rubbed green onto a white space. "I thought maybe he was a relative of Ingrid, or something. Say, what color is a giraffe?"

"Rela— why should Fidel Fundamento be a relative of Ingrid?" Bob demanded.

"Well," Jennifer replied sharply, "if two people are named the same they *could* be relatives, couldn't they? What's so dumb about that?"

"I didn't say it was dumb. Just tell me what you mean?"

"What I mean? What I mean? I mean Ingrid Fundamento and your friend must——"

"Ingrid Fundamento!" Bob cried. "Is her name Fundamento? Mom, is that right?"

"Well, let me see. I never did know for sure, but I thought her name was Ingrid Grundy."

"No, Mother." Jennifer insisted. "It's Annie Grundy and Ingrid Fundamento. I got their names the day they told me about the Arawak Indians. The dirty smugglers!"

Bob jumped up. "Do you understand, Mom?

They must be Fidel's contact! This means they're not racketeers—they're spies! Why didn't I see it before this?"

"Because I didn't tell you, that's why," Jennifer snapped.

"Excuse me, excuse me." Bob stumbled over the feet of other passengers as he hurried out to find Professor Narkus. Out on deck he found that the weather had taken a turn for the worse. Not only had the fog become so thick that he could barely see from one end of the vessel to the other—but it was drizzling.

Groping his way forward Bob found the Professor, with several others, staring intently into the pea soup ahead. He excitedly repeated what he had learned, the clue that tied the knitters in with Fidel.

"Sahih? Ya seh!" he exclaimed in Arabic. "So that's it. The submarine was really waiting for Fidel and his rubber boat, but the knitters went instead, when they learned that the spy had failed in his mission. That ties Fidel in with Tierra Ninguno. That will help in the investigation, all right. But we still have to nail down some evidence of espionage, and with the knitting ladies escaped, it's going to be *muy difícil*."

During the conversation, Bob was aware that the Professor had not given up staring into the mist ahead. Nothing could be seen. The *Clermont* was cruising slowly through the silence. Bob looked back to see his father lifting his eye patch to get a better view. Bob saw by his watch that they had been out more than thirty minutes, meaning that they should be raising Sandy Neck any moment.

A quarter-hour later Professor Narkus called to Captain Fulton in the pilothouse. "Where are we, Captain?"

"Right on course," came the confident reply.

Just then a shape loomed ahead. The *Clermont* crept closer. It was a long, pointed object that gradually emerged as a red-and-white marker. It slid by.

"Say, Dad, that's an open sea buoy, not a channel marker. We must be out of the harbor."

"Why, lad, you wouldn't have me come close to the dangerous reefs of Sandy Neck in this weather, would ye? Never be too cautious, that's my motto."

The drizzle and mist swirled around the vessel and its anxious passengers. Another fifteen minutes had gone by when another object suddenly appeared dead ahead in the fog.

"Land ho!" Captain Fulton yelled.

Bob was sure they were not near land. He squinted to identify the strange shape, which

"Land Ho!"

was now very close. It was a huge, glistening form stretching at great length across the *Clermont*'s course. Two tall spires shot upward from the center and disappeared into the mist above. Almost at once the group huddled on the bow of the ferry recognized it as a submarine. They gasped in amazement.

"Ein unterseeboot!" cried Professor Narkus.

A few feet more and even Captain Fulton realized what it was.

"Blast me barnacles!" he cried through the open port of the wheelhouse. "That's it! That's the sub that hijacked us! They're armed!"

As he spoke, men tumbled from the conning tower of the craft, which was now within spitting distance of the ferryboat. They seemed to be rushing to the five-inch gun on deck.

"Full speed astern!" shouted Captain Fulton. He grabbed the telegraph and notified the engine room. But in his nervousness, he signaled to Mr. Bones three short bells instead of one long jingle. Following orders, the engineer pushed the lever and sent the *Clermont* knifing ahead toward the hull of the dreadful ship!

21. An Encounter at Sea

A lot happened in the next few seconds. The *Clermont* raced directly at the sub. Captain Fulton hastily corrected his wrong signal to the engine room, but reversing the propeller did not make much difference in the onward rush of the steamer. He spun the wheel to the left and the ferry responded. The bow just missed the undersea craft, presenting her starboard beam to it.

The gun crew, in the meantime, had loaded their weapon and were now standing back, ready to fire. Bob saw one man hold the lanyard, another man raise his arm, and a third man cover his ears with his hands. The muzzle of the gun was aimed directly at the *Clermont*.

The knot of people on the foredeck of the ferryboat were yelling instructions to Captain Fulton or insults at the enemy on the other vessel. Several passengers had flattened themselves on the deck. Only the Captain seemed to know what to do.

"Pirates!" he shouted, pointing his shotgun out the pilothouse window and taking direct aim at the leader of the gun crew. "Surrender!"

The gun captain froze as he looked a few feet away at the steamboat slipping sideways toward him and saw the Captain pointing the muzzle of the shotgun at him. He hesitated, but only for a moment. He turned back to his men and was about to shout the order, "Fire!"

But he was too late. Just then the *Clermont* struck the submarine broadside with a crash. Those who were standing were thrown to the deck. That included the gun crew, and it also included Captain Fulton. As he fell, his shotgun discharged with a roar that seemed to break Bob's eardrums. He looked and saw that the three enemy seamen were now hugging *their* deck, for they knew they were under fire.

"Quick!" Bob cried to his father. "Keep them covered!" He grabbed a line and leaped to the sub, where he made the line fast. The noise and crash had brought most everyone out of the ferryboat cabin. Bob called for another line and made the stern fast to the sub, so the ships were tied up together.

The shotgun was again trained on the gunners, but now a head appeared at the conning tower. Bob shouted to Professor Narkus to alert the two security policemen who were escorting Fidel. One of these men hurried over to the sub and guarded the hatchway from which the sub's crew began to climb.

As each man came out, he was herded to the afterdeck of the sub while the Captain held his double-barreled weapon on the gang of unshaven, sullen men. There were eighteen in all. Then, to Bob's surprise, a familiar head appeared at the conning tower. Another popped up beside it. The knitters! Ingrid and Annie! The security cop ordered them down. They shuffled along the steel deck, crying and sobbing.

Half an hour later the scene was this: the main cabin had been cleared of passengers and was turned into a brig. In it were the sub's crew, the commander, the knitters, Fidel, the security police, Professor Narkus, Bob, Captain Fulton, and several officials from SNURP.

Outside, the fog was lifting, but the Coast Guard, on receiving the *Clermont*'s radio message of the matter, requested the ship to stand by. The submarine commander was bowing and addressing Captain Fulton. "Ah, my friend, we meet again, I see. Congratulations on your bravery, instructing me to pass to the RIGHT of Buoy No. 12 that day. Thanks to my stupidity and your cleverness, we ran aground. We have been here a fortnight, running low on supplies." His eyes flashed at his gun lieutenant. "If this idiot had done his job, we would have been out to sea on your fine steamboat by now."

Captain Fulton sneered, "Why, you blighters, you wouldn't have a clam's chance of getting away with it. You racketeers are going to the pokey for a stretch, that's what."

Professor Narkus said, *"Nyet, nyet,* sir, these are not racketeers, they are foreign agents."

Ingrid and Annie huddled in the corner, sniffling. Fidel had not spoken to them. He was handcuffed still. He just glared at Bob and the Professor.

Bob spoke to him. "All right, Fidel Fundamento, we know you and these women are in cahoots. Now, why don't you make it easy for yourself and tell us about your little spy ring."

Fidel scowled and laughed silently. Bob stared back at the black-clad fellow for a few seconds, and then his eyes widened. "Say, Professor," he said, "do you notice anything unusual about the sweater he's wearing?"

Everyone crowded around. The spy bent over, attempting to hide his garment. The security police pulled him back and Bob pointed to his chest. There seemed to be a beautifully executed and complicated design woven into the sweater.

"Why, there's Phinney's Lane!" exclaimed the Captain.

"This is Sandy Neck!" Bob traced another figure with his finger.

"Off with that sweater!" ordered the Professor.

They pulled the sweater off the sneering spy and held it up to the light. The pattern went completely around from one side to the other; it was a map of the area. At one strategic spot there was a clearly knit design of a tuba case. This was what had enabled the spy to find his way to the harbor, and to the garage.

"Who made this sweater, fella?" demanded the Captain.

"Why, there's only one person or persons who could have made this sweater!" Bob replied. He turned to point out Ingrid and Annie. They were just disappearing out the cabin door, for the guards had relaxed their vigil as they studied the sweater. "Quick, grab 'em!"

"Who made this sweater, fella?"

Ingrid and Annie were seized just as they were about to throw their knitting bags overboard. Inside the cabin, the contents of the bags were dumped on the table. In the mass of needles, yarn, tape measures, thread, and other junk were the makings of several kinds of knitted goods.

The amazed group found that Ingrid's shawl was a pretty design of nutmegs, sassafras trees, ginger, lemons, and so on.

"Hey, the Zeta-plus formula!" Bob cried.

Annie was working on a sweater which no one could figure out immediately. Suddenly, Professor Narkus said, "My goodness, that's our new antigravity tube! How did she get this?"

Captain Fulton asked, "You mean, they're really not racketeers after all?"

"Afraid not," the Professor replied. "We've got enough evidence, with these knitted messages, as it were, to convict the lot of them of espionage."

"They were sending secret orders to the agents in Tierra Ninguno," Bob said, "and all the time we thought they were helping the poor starving Arawak Indians. And there just isn't any such thing as an Arawak Indian any more."

"Jus' a meenit, my fran'," said a voice. Fidel was talking at last. He stood up straight. "I an' my seester Eengreed are two-thirds Arawak Eendian. We are ze last of our tribe. And some day we shall get back ze land and property zat ees rightfully ours. Some day we shall——"

"Oh, *fermez la bouche!*" ordered the Professor. "If you're Arawak Indians, at least you won't be starving any more. They'll feed you three times a day where you're going."

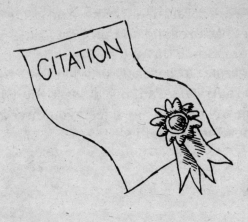

22. A Happy Decision

It wasn't long before the gray form of a Coast Guard cutter appeared. The prisoners were transferred to the ship to be taken to federal prison in Boston to await further investigation and the filing of criminal charges. A prize crew was put aboard the submarine, which was towed off the muddy shoal that had held it for the past two weeks.

Captain Fulton took his position at the helm of the *Clermont,* preparing to complete his voyage to Sandy Neck and the ceremonies which would now be held rather late due to the exciting events of the morning.

"Slow ahead," he called, signaling to the engine room. He squinted ahead. The fog had partially lifted, but there was nothing but ocean on all sides of him. "Now, let's see."

Bob entered the wheelhouse, knowing his father was lost. "Dad," he said quietly, "use the Automatic Pilot and Range Finder I installed." He pointed to the chart on the navigator's table. "Look. We're at Obstruction Buoy No. 12, right? Our course for Sandy Neck is 220 true, right? Well"—he turned a knob, adjusted a couple of dials and switches—"you just set this at 220 and turn this timer to here, and it'll bring us right into Bell Buoy No. 2 at the mouth of Sandy Neck channel."

That's exactly what it did.

The ceremony was held a couple of hours late. An unexpected part was hurriedly added at the end, when Captain Fulton was given a Special Citation for his bravery and fine seamanship in aiding in the capture of the spy ring. It said, in part:

"... who sailed fearlessly in the face of enemy gunfire ... ramming the enemy vessel without hesitation ... deliberately misleading enemy commander in giving him an escape route ... etc., etc."

Back home that night, Mrs. Fulton and Jennifer heard more details from Bob and the Captain.

"How did Ingrid get the formula?" Bob's mother asked.

"They were in the garage the day I jotted it down on my yellow pad of paper. She was looking at it and knitting it right into her shawl, I guess. Memorized most of it, probably."

"When did they swipe the Zeta-plus that the Constable thought was jam?"

"The day you had Ingrid to tea. That's all I can figure out. Annie wasn't there, so she must have been out in the garage."

"Well, they're certainly a couple of smart cookies," Captain Fulton observed.

Mrs. Fulton stood before the mantel and studied the awards her family had won that day. "I guess the real smart cookies are right here in this room," she smiled.

"That's right," Jennifer piped up. The others looked strangely at her, not knowing whether she really referred to herself as a smart cooky. The Fulton family went to bed that night tired and full of exciting thoughts about the hours, days, weeks, and months of the past.

But the future had not been entirely settled. The following morning Captain Fulton chewed on his blubber steak and thought about his son.

He had proven to his father's satisfaction that he was talented as a sailor and as a scientist. That much the summer had accomplished. But which course should the boy follow? The Captain decided to let the young man make up his own mind.

After breakfast the two of them stood in the sunlit driveway and discussed it. "Son, now that school's open again, you got to be plannin' a course for your future. I'd say ye proved your mettle in several ways. Now, I'm going to let ye make up your own mind."

"To tell the truth, Dad," the boy replied, "all that's happened this summer has made it tougher for me. Now I think the sea has as much to offer as science. I wish I could do both."

Just then the slim figure of Professor Narkus came down the lane to catch the first boat to the Neck. He greeted the Fultons.

Captain Fulton told the Professor about Bob's ambitions. He also mentioned his own hopes for his son.

Bob looked at the Professor, who rubbed his fingers up and down on his cheek. He grimaced. Apparently he was thinking heavily. The other two watched him silently. Then he spoke.

"Gentlemen," he declared, "do you realize where the great unexplored areas of the universe lie? Do you know where the tremendous, un-bounded treasures of the world are to be found? Do you know where, in abundance, are virtually unlimited supplies of practically every mineral which we need for our existence? Do you know where, by careful research and exploration, we can find the answers to mysteries of the great cosmos that surrounds us? Do you know what makes up three-fifths of the earth we live on, and yet nine-tenths of which we are ignorant about?"

The Fultons gaped, unable to answer.

"The oceans, my friends. There are those of us who believe that our space experiments will come to an end some day, and that surpassing them in importance will be the science of oceanography. You, my boy, can become a scientist and a sailor at one and the same time. Not as a freak, but to ride the wave of the future!"

Bob's face broke into a huge grin.

Captain Fulton's eye sparkled. "Blimy! What a scheme! Robert Farragut Fulton, scientist of the seven seas. And the first thing you can do is make yourself a snorkel so's you can swim the harbor under water and pay off that bet we made! Ho! Ho! Ho!"

---

23. Epilogue

Bob Fulton went back to school that fall with some memories of a summer he would never forget. He also could see a future which made sense to him and for which he could prepare.

The town of Barnstable finally settled down. Soon it got to the point where the Pop Stretcher seemed a part of the landscape. Men were being shot into space, into orbit, and on toward the moon and planets. The excitement of these events often obscured the interesting fact that without the peculiar discoveries of a young man named Bob Fulton, the conquest of space would have been more difficult and a longer time coming.

One of the most fascinating developments came from the discovery that the knitting ladies had dispatched a jar of Zeta-plus to Tierra Ninguno. At the trial, the three spies gloated over this fact. Nevertheless, because their espionage activities had not really hurt the United States, they were given suspended sentences and deported to their native land.

Back in Tierra Ninguno, they were able to supply the scientists there with enough piecemeal information so that eventually a Pop Stretcher was constructed. Using the jar of authentic material, they were able to get a Zeta-plus manufacturing effort going.

The revolutionary government of Tierra Ninguno decided to throw all its resources behind this operation. Since the sugar production of the country was fifteen times as great as that of the United States, it was quite some time before the candy shortage became serious.

For a period of time, Tierra Ninguno enjoyed tremendous prosperity, using all its sugar and turning out Zeta-plus for its own purposes as well as for all the countries of the world that were willing to buy it.

Then came the candy famine. Although everyone's bicycle had frictionless bearings, and no one had to wind his watch, and the trains ran for

*They were given suspended sentences and
deported to their native land.*

days on one tank of diesel oil, people became terribly restless.

One day they marched against the palace, overthrew the existing regime, and installed a People's Party. The first act of the People's Party was to destroy the Pop Stretcher.

It was obvious, then, that the world was not ready for frictionless bearings. The people still preferred sweets.

ABOUT THE AUTHOR

JEROME BEATTY has written five books for adults and thirteen books for young readers, the best known being the *Matthew Looney* series. He wrote "Trade Winds" column for the *Saturday Review* for thirteen years and has written articles and humor for many magazines such as the *Reader's Digest, Esquire, Redbook, McCalls,* etc. Beatty and his wife have four daughters and live in Falmouth, Massachusetts.

ABOUT THE ILLUSTRATOR

GAHAN WILSON's work is syndicated worldwide and appears in *Playboy, New Yorker,* the *National Lampoon, Audubon, Punch, Gourmet, Paris Match,* and *Esquire* as well as on the Op-Ed page of *The New York Times.*

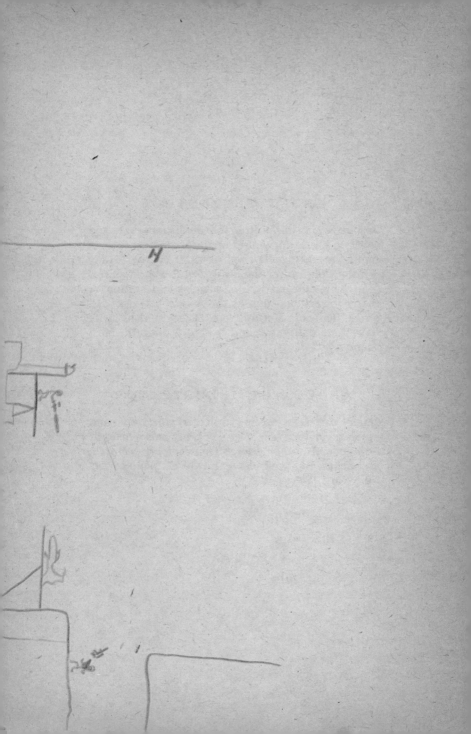